MELTING POINT

By

Cleo Dare

Women's Work Press, LLC
P.O. Box 10375 Burke, Virginia 22009-0375

Printed in the United States of America
First Edition

Library of Congress Card Number: 2001097738

ISBN 1-930874-03-0

DEDICATION

For Chris,

A quarter century is not enough, let's shoot for half this time!

And,

With a nod to Josephine Tey

ABOUT THE AUTHOR...

A photographer and videographer, Cleo Dare has been roaming the western United States for the past 15 years. "I'm a very visual person and I love to travel to immerse myself in the unique beauty of other landscapes, other cultures, other lifeways."

One of Cleo's ambitions is to visit every national and state park in the United States. The other is to go back to school to complete a master's degree in women's studies.

She is an aficionado of motorcycling, rollerblading, nature sketching, and jazz. Cleo's current home base is in New Mexico and her main goal in life, despite her demanding ambitions, is to "enjoy each moment to the fullest."

As if in a dream, Kelly entered a world where the ephemera of another woman's ghost lingered. She hadn't expected it, but it didn't surprise her, either. Kelly felt the ghost rush toward her, but she could do nothing to resist it. The ghost recognized her and knew why she had come.

She heard the ghost's secret cry of victory and then felt it suffuse the fresh emptiness of her lungs and rise like a soft exhaled mist into her mind. It wasn't painful or frightening. It was inevitable. She was truly Nancy now.

Other than the ghost, which had been subsumed into Kelly in a moment that existed outside of time and which neither of the men could have perceived, Kelly Bransford saw nothing in the room Dave Paxton had helped her to memorize except Jim Summerhill's pained old blue eyes lifting to meet hers.

"Dad," she said.

ONE

"He's running the business into the ground, Jim."

"There's nothing I can do." Jim's hands rested limply on the black plastic arms of his wheelchair. His neck was held upright with a thick white brace.

"Yes, there is, damn it. Get rid of him."

"One more rejection, Dave, and that boy is going to snap."

Dave Paxton, the accountant for Summerhill Foundry, paced in the cramped linoleum-floored room that was Jim Summerhill's office. "I don't see that, Jim. Listen to me as a friend. Your oldest friend."

Dave stopped pacing and looked down at the wrecked body of a man he had know for nearly 25 years. *Damn that drunken asshole driver! How many times a day did Dave say that to himself? And why did he bother? It didn't change anything.*

"All right."

"Walter's not happy here. He doesn't have any artistic talent, and little business talent. Rose shows him up in both areas with an ease that has to be hard on his ego. If anything, it's failing at a business he doesn't understand that's going to make him snap."

Jim blinked. "So why does he stay on?"

"So he can skim as much money off the top as he can get away with. When I blow a gasket, he stops pilfering, but not for long."

Jim's eyes closed in pain.

"The only thing he cares about is sailing on Cochiti Lake. You know it and I know it, Jim. He's a mimbo."

Jim opened his eyes and let out an exasperated sigh. "I've always known Walter was a mimbo, Dave. That's why I was going to leave the business to Nancy. If she was here—"

"I know. The foundry would be running smooth as glass and turning a profit, too."

"If only I could still cast—" A shine of tears edged the old man's eyes and he could do nothing to shake them off or wipe them away. "Damn it. All I can do anymore is bitch and moan."

"Bitching and moaning is good." A wiry petite woman with friendly wrinkle lines covering every inch of her weathered face came into the room. "But now it's almost time for lunch."

"Thanks, Alice. Is Dave invited?"

"Of course."

But Dave shook his head. "I have to meet another client downtown for lunch." He smiled apologetically at Alice. "I'd much rather have your home cooking."

"Oh, pooh," she disagreed, wheeling Jim's chair around, "some of the best restaurants in the whole United States are in downtown Santa Fe."

"The most expensive ones, too," Dave shot back. Jim and Alice laughed.

Dave drifted around the Santa Fe Plaza, picking the remains of his tamale from his teeth. His business with Adobe Constructs had finished early and the lazy summer afternoon enticed him to play hookey. There was an art fair under way and the colorful booths of hopeful unknowns lined the sidewalks, inviting Santa Fe's endless torrent of summer tourists to view their wares.

Dave's artistic tastes ran to the quirky and unique, and if something amused him, he bought it. He had covered three sides of the Plaza without anything catching his eye when he was so startled he spoke out loud: "Nancy—"

Dave clapped a hand over his mouth. *No, it couldn't be.*

A twenty-something artist exhibiting kiln-fired pottery sculptures of domestic animals in cute and clever poses was a dead ringer for Jim's lost daughter. Dave forced himself to look away.

Undoubtedly, his unconscious was obsessing over the problems of his old friend Jim and the fiscal health of the foundry. That had to be why the woman looked so much like Nancy Summerhill to him. He was ascribing qualities to this woman that had been brought back to his memory when Jim mentioned Nancy earlier that morning.

He looked again, feeling only a shade calmer. The young woman was showing a whimsical sculpture of cats tumbling to a pair of tourists. While she gestured and spoke, Dave catalogued the remarkable physical similarities between her and the Nancy he remembered. He guessed she was around 5'4" tall and had a husky but not a bulky, figure. Her dark brunette hair was cut short in a bob and her hazel eyes laughed as she worked at charming her customers.

Her cheekbones were wide and high and her chin firm with

character, all Summerhill characteristics. But surely, Dave told himself, it was only a passing resemblance. One of those peculiarities of light and shadow. Besides, how could he know what Nancy Summerhill would look like now anyway?

When she had disappeared at age seventeen along with a girlfriend, Barbara Knox, her hair had been long, almost down to her waist. That had been seven years ago. Nancy would be twenty-four now.

Was this woman twenty-four? Dave stared hard at her but he could only guess at her age. She could be 24 or she could be 30.

The tourist couple had decided on a sculpture of two terriers leaping for the same ball and the artist was writing out a receipt of sale. Dave hesitated, unsure whether to move on or try to make the woman's acquaintance.

He shrugged mentally and stepped into her booth. What did he have to lose? While she wrote out a bill of sale for her customers, he pretended to be absorbed in studying a sculpture of a cockatoo smoking a cigar. Out of the corner of his eye, he saw her hand over a bubble-wrapped parcel of the terriers to her customers. Then she turned abruptly on him.

"Why were you staring at me?" Her voice was throaty. Although more mature than he remembered it, the woman's voice was eerily reminiscent of Nancy's. Dave was so startled, his arm jerked and he knocked the cockatoo from its base. It fell, shattering on the pavement.

"Fuck!" The woman cursed. She charged toward him, flailing her arms to push him away. "Get out of here or I'm calling the cops!"

"I'm sorry!" Dave leaped backward. "I didn't mean any harm. It was an accident."

"Get out of here!" The woman set her jaw and an angry

dimple protruded from her chin. Dave, despite his chagrin, was even more flabbergasted. He had seen Nancy's dimple do exactly that on many an aggravated childhood occasion...*My god,* he thought, *this woman has to be Nancy*!

"Nancy—" he implored, reaching his hand toward her. The woman blocked his arm with a hard slam of her fist to his wrist. "Get out of my booth!"

At the same moment Dave felt pain radiate up his arm, a pair of hands locked onto each side of his belt at his waist. "C'mon, man, do as the lady says." There was a backward tug on his waistband.

Dave raised his hands in surrender. "All right, all right." He backed out of the booth with the other man, who released him.

"Sorry," Dave apologized. He turned to see a slender Hispanic man who was younger and a good foot shorter than himself. The man was dressed in a muscle shirt and tight blue jeans. "It was just a misunderstanding."

"These things happen," the man agreed, "but even out here on neutral ground, I'd be a little afraid of her." He shrugged a shoulder in the young artist's direction. "She looks like she's ready to charge you."

"I'll stay a safe distance," Dave said. "Thanks again."

"Sure. Good luck."

Dave turned his attention away from the young man and looked at the woman he had christened Nancy. Her hands were on her hips and her nostrils were practically flaring. "What the fuck do you want, anyway?"

"I want to pay for the piece I broke. Just tell me how much it is and I'll put the money right here on the ground and then I'll walk away. Okay?"

"Okay. It's $75." The woman crossed her arms over her chest. Dave pulled a $100 bill from his wallet and laid it on the ground.

"That's too much," the woman retorted instantly. *Abrupt, direct, precise,* Dave categorized. Every quality was a classic quality of Nancy's. But Nancy was dead and he couldn't imagine who this woman could be. She looked like Nancy, she sounded like Nancy...and she didn't recognize him.

Nancy would have recognized him instantaneously, no matter how great the passage of years. He had been there for her birth, her christening, her first school play, her sweet sixteen birthday party.

He was the one in whom Nancy had confided that she had fallen in love with Barbara Knox. She had confided in him because she knew he was gay and she had wanted his blessing. He had given it... and then she had up and vanished into thin air.

"I don't have any change," Dave said, careful to keep any hint of challenge from his voice.

"I think I've got a twenty and a five," the woman replied, reaching for her cashbox.

"Why don't you keep the difference?" Dave suggested. "You know, for all the bother I've caused. And also, I like that prancing horse."

"Which one?" The woman's head turned to view her stock.

"The one with the aqua saddle and the black hooves." Dave gestured with his chin, careful not to make any abrupt moves that might upset her.

"Prancer. She's $135."

"So, $100 and $135...that's $235."

"$210," the woman corrected. "Shorty was only $75, remember?"

"Look," Dave repeated, "I'm sorry. It really was an accident."

"Then why were you staring at me?" The woman sat down on a tall stool and cradled her cashbox protectively on her knees.

"You look exactly—and I mean exactly—like someone I used

to know. Someone I really cared for." Dave's voice pleaded for understanding.

"A girlfriend? A wife?"

"No. I'm gay." *What the heck,* Dave thought to himself, *he couldn't get into any deeper water at this point.* "She was like...like a daughter to me. The daughter I would have wanted to have."

The woman's eyebrows quirked and Dave felt like he'd been slugged in the stomach by the familiarity of the look. "What happened to her?"

Dave's throat was dry. "She disappeared about seven years ago."

"Is she dead?"

"I thought so...until I saw you today. It was a shock."

The woman shifted the cashbox on her knees and opened the lid, starting to search for change. "Look, I'm sorry. I thought you were trying to pick me up and then you broke Shorty—"

"I understand. It was too much."

"I haven't sold very much here today..." Her head dropped and her boot kicked at the rungs of the stool.

"Well," Dave suggested, "how about I pay you for Shorty and Prancer and you let me take you out to dinner? To make up for the lousy day."

The woman's head shot up and her face flushed with anger. She slammed shut the cashbox lid. Her jaw was set in a hard line again, the dimple making its reappearance. "I wanna see your gay card, mister, 'cause I can tell you right now, if you don't have one, this is the most elaborate pick-up routine I've ever seen a guy pull. Even an older, more desperate kind of guy."

"Hey..." Dave was flummoxed. *Jeez, was his hair getting that gray?*

"I mean it, buddy! Produce."

"Shit," Dave exhaled. "Okay." He unbuttoned his left sleeve

and rolled it up. Hidden on the fleshy inside of his bicep was a small red tattoo of a pair of intimately-coupled arrow-topped circles—the ancient Greek symbol for Mars—and a modern hieroglyphic for homosexual men.

"It's my only tattoo," he muttered in annoyance, rolling his sleeve back down, "and I try to keep it hidden. Especially from people who aren't likely to turn out to be lovers. If you get my drift."

"I get it. But it's a damn good thing you have it. It just came in real handy. Now, where exactly are you taking me to dinner?"

They sat outdoors on the rooftop patio of Pranzo's Italian Grill. The buzz of an occasional car and the conversations and laughter of foot traffic drifted up to them from the street. Kelly Bransford could just make out the melancholy strains of the blues trio that was playing in the open patio of Cowgirl Hall of Fame half a block away.

Never in her wildest dreams would Kelly have expected to find herself sharing a gourmet dinner with an older man atop the roof of a swank downtown restaurant. Unlike the well-to-do who reveled in Santa Fe's pricey southwestern ambience, Kelly would have expected to be where she had been for the last week at this hour of the day: stretched out on the peeling vinyl seat of her rusting Ford pickup, one hand pillowed under her head and the other loosely gripping the truck's tire iron. She hoped she would never need to use the tire iron, but its closeness to hand gave her a much-needed sense of security, however false.

She had seriously considered getting a dog for protection,

but in the end she had decided she couldn't afford to feed a dog and it would have proved impossible, not to mention inhumane, to keep an animal locked up in the truck for long periods of time.

She parked her truck in a different parking lot or space every night to sleep, keeping to the downtown area because with all the summer tourist traffic it felt safer. Of course, that also meant the area was more heavily-patrolled by cops, but so far she'd only been asked to move once. The Hispanic officer, after checking out her Colorado driver's license, had been—except for the avuncular crack about getting a boyfriend—perfectly pleasant to her.

The bed of her truck was covered with a sturdy and lockable aluminum top but it was impossible to sleep in the bed because it was packed cheek by jowl with her art pieces. Without her pieces, she was nowhere and nothing.

"You seem preoccupied," Dave said, his fingers twirling the stem of his wine glass.

"Just admiring the view," Kelly said. "It's...heavenly."

Dave smiled. "Glad you like it. It's one of my favorite restaurants."

"Do you eat out often?"

Dave desperately wanted to get past the small talk but he had resigned himself to bear it. Also, now that the Nancy look-alike had introduced herself as Kelly Bransford, itinerant artist, he was unsure what he wanted to say.

"Yes, but I'm an accountant." He laughed. "I don't usually have to pay."

Kelly straightened. "You said—"

"Calm down." He fluttered his hand. "The tab's on me as we agreed."

"I don't want to seem rude," Kelly said, "but what are we

doing? I mean, I look like someone you once knew. Big deal. It isn't much in the way of the basis for starting a relationship and I don't—"

Dave focused on Kelly's hesitation. "You don't what?"

"—establish relationships with men."

Dave leaned forward. "Are you saying what I think you're saying?"

"What am I saying?"

"Are you saying you're *family*?"

Kelly nodded. "I've known since I was a little girl."

"Shit."

"Hey, you're queer yourself. Don't go and get self-righteous on me."

"Nan—I mean, Kelly, it's not self-righteousness. It's just...it's just so utterly unbelievable."

"Okay, okay, I get it. This Nancy person was gay too, wasn't she?"

Dave gulped. "Yes, she was. Or at least she thought she was. She was only seventeen when—"

"—she died. You told me already."

Dave's face paled.

Kelly frowned. She was getting annoyed with all the pent up mystery. "She did die, right?"

"Well, her body was never found. We *assumed* she died."

"Look," Kelly said, "I've already told you that I'm not her."

"I know. I know you're not her." Dave moved his wine glass aside as a heaping plate of fettucine alfredo was placed in front of him by the waiter. "You just look like her. You look so much like her—"

Kelly's platter of chicken marsala, meat lasagna, and prawns in cream sauce was set down and her attention was diverted by the sheer grandeur of her meal. She had been living on a diet of fast food burritos, corn chips and chemical-sludge coffee for so long she had forgotten gourmet cooking or even home cooking existed.

She took a deep whiff of her plate and then, lifting a forkful of prawns, laid them on her tongue with reverence. They were divine. She had forgotten Dave existed until five bites later when she looked up from her absorption to see him watching her.

"I, uh—" she flushed with embarrassment. She guessed she was behaving like someone who'd never seen food before.

"You," Dave raised his napkin to his mouth, "are enjoying your meal to the full."

"Yes. I—"

"You don't have to explain."

"Thanks," she said sheepishly. She slipped another bite of meltingly-rich lasagna into her mouth. "Weren't you saying something when our plates arrived? I got distracted."

"A thought was forming in my mind. A very strange thought."

"Oh brother. It's back to this Nancy thing. You think I'm lying about not being Nancy."

"No. I know you're telling the truth. You've made that clear and, unless you're suffering from an extraordinary case of amnesia, you're somebody else."

"Exactly. So, what was your thought?"

"My thought was you could *be* Nancy."

Kelly frowned. "Aren't you just playing with words now? I'm not Nancy."

"What I'm saying is you could *pretend to be* Nancy."

"Why in heaven's name would I want to do that?"

"Actually, quite a few reasons come to mind." Dave twirled strands of fettucine on his fork.

"This is crazy! You are a crazy person! I mean, I appreciate the dinner and everything—" she looked down at what remained of it with a wary look, as if it would bite her— "but you are certifiable, Dave. If Dave is even your real name."

"I could show you my business card, Kelly. If Kelly is even your real name."

Kelly half-rose from her chair. "I'm getting steamed here, Dave."

"Sit down, Kelly. You haven't even heard what I'm thinking yet."

"It's bound to be illegal. Impersonation is illegal." She was standing, her arms crossed over her chest.

Dave shrugged. "It's for a good cause."

"Good cause? What cause?"

"Healing an old man's heart and saving a floundering business."

TWO

Dawn was only a shimmer of pale pink light limning the Sangre de Cristo mountains but Kelly was already wide awake. The wine she had drunk the night before had lulled her into a deep sleep the moment her head touched the seat of her truck, but now she was nervously alert, eyeing the empty street.

Even after just three glasses of wine, she had decided to err on the side of caution and not move her truck from the meter at which it was parked when she went to dinner with Dave. She was on Alameda Street, quite close to the narrow trickle of water which passed for the Santa Fe River. All was still quiet at this early hour and she longed for a cup of coffee.

Coffee would help her think. Coffee would clear the cobwebs from her brain and help her sort through the story Dave Paxton, C.P.A., had told her. In the light of day, everything would be clearer and she would be able to make a decision.

She turned the ignition and the cold engine of the Ford

ground. "Come on, baby," she whispered to it tenderly. The Ford ground some more and then sputtered into life. Kelly affectionately patted the steering wheel, worn down and cracked from years of use. She would have to let the old engine warm up for a few minutes before she slid the transmission into gear.

She shivered as she waited, snuggling deeper into her duct-tape-patched goose down coat. It was summer and the early morning cold would pass off soon. She reached for the pink comb she kept stashed in the glove compartment and pulled its teeth through the mass of tangles in her hair.

Where to get coffee? She wondered, gently pressing down the accelerator to keep the engine from dying out as it fought the notion of running so early in the cold morning. It was hard to imagine, after the *haute cuisine* she had enjoyed the previous evening, that she would be satisfied with a cup of the coffee sludge she'd been drinking from the downtown area's only gas station.

She lifted up her shoulders in wonderment. She had felt so spoiled last night: an appetizer of stuffed mushrooms and a red wine which she and Dave had shared followed by a mixed-green salad which the waiter had spiced with fresh ground pepper to her specifications. Next her elaborate combination meal with a lighter white wine; and finally a dessert of the softest, most exquisite chocolate torte, and a decaffeinated cappuccino with all the trimmings: whipped cream, cinnamon and chocolate curls.

She had taken Dave for everything she could. It was his fault, of course. She had been willing to be more judicious in her choices, but he had insisted at the outset that money was no object and she could order whatever she wanted.

She had wondered, of course, if she would owe him something for it. He had insisted otherwise. All he had asked was that she consider the proposition he had made to her. The bizarre proposition that she pretend to be a woman she had never met.

She slid the truck into gear and eased out of the parking space. She was not going to Corky's Fill 'Er Up this morning. She was going to one of Santa Fe's see-and-be-seen coffee hangouts where stars like Gene Hackman and Amy Irving wandered in for their cup of morning brew. Sure, the coffee would be three times as expensive but she needed to settle into a corner and think. Think hard for a very long time.

Dave Paxton's accounting office was located on the second floor of an old hacienda constructed around the courtyard of Sena Plaza. Before she headed up the ancient wooden stairs that led to the second floor balcony and a very strange future, Kelly had taken the precaution of calling the Santa Fe Better Business Bureau to find out if they knew anything shady or disreputable about Mr. Paxton or his business.

They didn't.

She had followed that call up with a call to the state's Board of Accountancy to determine if Mr. Paxton was in good standing with his licensing board.

He was.

Nor did they have any reports of any malfeasance of any kind on Mr. Paxton's part. Kelly had thanked them and hung up. As near as she could tell, the man was not known to cheat his clients, falsify audits, cook the books, or run scams.

At least, if he did, he had never been caught.

Even in this proposition he had made to her, she couldn't see what he had to gain financially. And he had made it clear he hadn't anything to gain. When she had asked him point blank about it, he had said: "A smile of pure happiness from Jim Summerhill is more than enough reward for me." He had leaned toward her then, across the table. "A single smile, after so many years of pain and regret and grief, Kelly."

Kelly shook off the memory of Dave's hazel eyes boring into her own with a depth of sincerity she didn't think possible to fake. He didn't, he claimed, own any proprietary or economic interest in Summerhill Foundry. He had admitted the only remotely fiscal benefit to him was that if the foundry survived, he retained a good client.

He had howled with laughter when she suggested that a sexual interest in Jim was his real motive and that perhaps Jim was too distraught over the state of the foundry to respond to his overtures.

"Why is that so funny?" She had questioned.

"Jim Summerhill is almost old enough to be my father, but aside from that, he's straight and he's a quadriplegic. Our relationship doesn't have anything to do with sex."

"What does it have to do with then?" She had demanded.

"When I was fifteen and my own father found out about me, he threw me out of the house. Suffice it to say, Jim Summerhill took me in, gave me a job, and later, helped me pay for college."

"But you've paid him back, right? I mean for college and everything." They had been lingering over their cappuccinos by that time.

Dave sighed. "Of course I've paid him back and I helped him raise Walter and Nancy after their mother died too, and done whatever else he needed, but I could never pay back what Jim did for me. You can never pay that kind of thing back, Kelly."

Kelly had refused to let her thoughts stray to her own family's stony disapproval of her. No one had extended such a welcome to her after her family's rejection and she had pushed along, desperate to survive most of the time, but owing no one. It wasn't that she didn't believe Dave, but his story sent a discomfiting shaft of jealousy through her chest.

"And despite this close relationship," she persisted, "you're not going to inherit? He's still going to will the foundry to Walter?"

"He's already willed the foundry to Walter."

"But aren't you, in a sense, his favorite son?"

"Yes, but, unfortunately, I'm not the son of his body and Jim, despite his quirks, remains a traditionalist."

"But originally he had willed it to his daughter Nancy?"

"Yes, because Nancy had the gift to make it great—a quality he didn't see in Walter—and he isn't so much of a traditionalist that he would deny Nancy just because she was a female."

"So, if I agree to this pretend stuff and everything goes smoothly, he might will the foundry to me?" Kelly's logic had been relentless and this is where Dave had hesitated the most. Finally he'd hedged: "I haven't thought that far along, Kelly. I'm just thinking about the financial health of the foundry, the immediate future—"

"But it could happen, couldn't it?"

"Yes," he'd admitted.

"And if that happened, we would be conspiring to steal the foundry from its rightful heir, Walter Summerhill."

Dave put his head in his hands. "Walter, left to his own devices, will have the place in bankruptcy in less than a year."

"It's still fraud. It's still theft."

"In a year, there won't be anything left to steal."

They had finished the evening at this impasse but Dave had still begged her to think it over. He had given her his card and told her to come by his office or call at any time.

When they rose from the table, she had, in an uncharacteristic moment of sentimentality, brushed his cheek with her lips and whispered in his ear, "It was an extraordinary, if strange, evening," before striding away in the darkness and walking, alone, to her truck.

Now, it was going on 11 in the morning and Kelly raised her foot to mount the shadowed stairs that led to Dave's office. The archaic wood of the treads had been worn down into wells. Off to her right, the summer sun filled the courtyard of Sena Plaza with bright innocence, magnifying the color of the summer flowers planted in the old stone fountain and gilding the glossy leaves of the patio trees. Tourists wandered in and out of the narrow blue-painted doors which fronted the shops that occupied the first floor.

Why was she doing this? she asked herself. Adventure, desperation, or just plain opportunity?

Earlier in the morning, at the coffee shop, she had watched the well-to-do, the artists, the smattering of stars, the gallery owners, and the inevitable tourists come and go.

She wanted, she realized then, to have a life more closely approximating theirs. A life where she wasn't wondering if she could afford the next taco or the next fill-up of gas. A life where she belonged. A life where she was someone.

A life where...what? A life where she was Nancy Summerhill? Her foot drew back from the first rung of the stairs, a visible manifestation of her uncertainty.

No, she reminded herself firmly. A life where she was an acknowledged artist, a businesswoman, a person through whom the pulse of the artistic community flowed. The Santa Fe artistic community, no less.

Every time Dave had used the word *foundry* the night before, she had trembled with excitement. That, more than anything else, had captured her imagination. If he'd been offering her a restaurant, she would have laughed in his face—and still accepted his offer of dinner.

But to cast her own clay pieces in bronze, to cast the work of others, to restore the Summerhill Foundry to its former reputation...the notion was full of heady intoxication and Dave, once he saw where her enthusiasm lay, had done a good job of selling it to her.

But to do it, she had to risk everything. She even had to throw away her true identity, change her name, and pretend to be someone she was not.

On the other hand, accepting Dave's offer would shave years off the starving artist's existence she was leading now: working at odd jobs to raise the fees for kiln-firing her pieces, finding barren wayside locations to set up her potting wheel and potting madly before a landowner caught her and threw her off his property, sleeping in her truck, meeting no one but fast food counter clerks and gas station cashiers.

If she pretended to be Nancy Summerhill, she would 'make it' that much faster and, in Santa Fe, of all places. Santa Fe, which was regarded as one of the unscalable Everests of the art world for so many hopeful artists like herself.

And what did her true identity matter anyway? At the moment, she was no one. She was an unknown, a blue collar kid from a wrong-side-of-the-tracks neighborhood in Pueblo, Colorado, an adopted child whose parents hadn't made that much of an investment in her to begin with and now, because of homophobia, no longer cared whether she lived or died, not to mention failed or succeeded.

So wasn't this deal, this impersonation, the greatest opportunity that had ever landed in her lap? What did it matter if people addressed her as 'Kelly' or 'Nancy'? Wasn't what she was going to be able to accomplish far more important than who she might have started out in life as? Hadn't dozens of famous successful people started out with other names, other identities, putting behind themselves murky backgrounds that didn't hold up to scrutiny?

The answer was obvious even if she quailed at the challenge rising before her. Kelly took a deep breath and mounted the dangerous stairs to her destiny.

THREE

Dave was, to say the least, ecstatic. He slapped his hands on the carved Spanish table that served as his desk and, jumping up, started to pace.

"I've been up all night thinking about this!"

"Thinking about whether or not I'd accept?"

"No. Figuring out how to get you trained without anyone finding out."

"Trained?"

"Kelly, you're going to need to know everything about Nancy, about the Summerhill family, about the foundry, even about Santa Fe. And we're going to have to create a plausible past that covers the years between Nancy's age of seventeen and right now. For instance, why are you coming back now? We have hundreds of questions to answer and thousands of details for you to memorize."

Kelly blanched. She had known this, of course, but hadn't

yet focused on what would actually have to be done.

Dave noticed her expression. "Are you still with me?"

"Yes," she said, only the faintest hint of hesitation in her voice. "When do we get started?"

In the end, Dave decided to put Kelly up in the duplex he owned as a *pied a terre* in Albuquerque, sixty miles to the south of Santa Fe. Dave had bought the duplex as an investment property because he had clients in Albuquerque and found himself in the city once or twice a week.

He often scheduled his business with his Albuquerque clients on Fridays or Mondays so he could party on the weekends in one of Albuquerque's gay bars. Not infrequently, he would bring a friend back to the duplex for a quieter and much more satisfying kind of partying.

With Kelly in residence he would have to temporarily suspend his regular weekend habits and spend all of that time coaching her for her new role. The good thing was, nothing noticeable in his routine would change: he would still be in Albuquerque on the weekends. He didn't have a secretary or a family in Santa Fe but he did have enough straight friends and colleagues who might notice a drastic alteration in his regular routine and wonder about it.

It was also safer for Kelly to be in Albuquerque where she wasn't likely to be recognized by anyone who knew the Summerhill family. He certainly didn't want her face becoming a familiar one around Santa Fe until she was fully versed in being Nancy.

Kelly agreed to meet him on the following Friday on the outskirts of Santa Fe and follow him to Albuquerque in her truck. He would show her the duplex and leave her to get settled.

"Do you have anything to move?" he asked.

"No. Everything's in my truck."

"Where are you staying now?"

"Truck," she said tersely.

He dipped his head in consternation, but proceeded without comment. "Pets?"

"Nope."

"All right, then."

"Wait," Kelly raised a hand. "There is the small matter of money, Dave. If I'm not potting, firing, and traveling to art shows—"

"Well, obviously the rent's free. But I'll give you a weekly stipend in addition—in cash—until we get you settled into a position at the foundry. You can use it to buy groceries and whatever else you need."

"Can I set up my potter's wheel?"

"Of course. But if you want anything fired, I'll have to take it somewhere in Albuquerque. I don't want people seeing you. Which reminds me, you'd better start signing your work with Nancy's initials. Can you re-sign your current pieces?"

"I'm not sure, but I might be able to sand out my old initials. Did Nancy have a middle initial? And would she have used it?"

"Yes. Her middle name was Arlene, for Jim's sister Arlene, who was killed in a car crash just a few months before Nancy was born. Jim was on a tour of duty overseas at the time so he wasn't even able to come home for his sister's funeral. He did make it home for Nancy's birth, though. Nancy's mother died when Nancy was five and Walter was four. By then, Jim was home again and trying to make the foundry work. He was only too happy to get out of the service."

"Where were you during all of this?"

"I was in college in Albuquerque."

Kelly nodded. "Okay, so, Nancy's full name was Nancy Arlene Summerhill, right?"

"Right."

"NAS. Okay. I'll try to change it on my pieces."

"What else?" Dave looked up at the dark wood ceiling, deep in thought.

"What about the neighbors —I mean, your tenants—in the other half of the duplex?"

"Oh, Ralph and Charlie. They own a hairdressing business and are outrageous queens at work, but at home they live a very quiet monogamous life. You can be Kelly Bransford with them. I'll just tell them you're a distant cousin who needed a safe place to dry out and get her life back together."

"Dry out? That isn't very complimentary, you know. I've never had any kind of drug or alcohol abuse problem."

"Well, you're too old to have run away from your parents. What do you suggest?"

Kelly waved her hand dismissively. "I guess it'll have to do."

"Do you cook and clean?"

"Of course, but I'm not cleaning up after you."

"I wouldn't expect you to. It's not part of the deal."

"What is part of the deal?"

"You lie low during the week, memorizing what I teach you and we cram every weekend until you're absolutely ready. We don't spring you on the foundry until every last *t* is crossed and every *i* dotted. Until you are Nancy in your own head. Got it?"

"Got it."

Dave looked into Kelly's face, his expression concerned. "Kelly, look. This is your last chance to back out, so..."

"No, Dave. Friday at 8 am is my last chance to back out. If you don't see my truck at the Interstate 25 exit, you'll know I took a powder. But, until then—" Kelly stood and sketched him a wave, "—*adios*, Dave."

Being someone else was not as weird as Kelly had thought it would be. The method of rote memorization she and Dave had been employing wasn't all that different from the immersion method of learning a foreign language.

After three months of immersion, Kelly was beginning to think and dream in Nancy. She was beginning to believe she had Nancy's past. She knew she wasn't Nancy, but she could appreciate Nancy's upbringing and Nancy's experiences in a way that made it easy to adopt them as her own. She didn't know what Nancy had felt on the inside, and never would, but she was beginning to relate to her as though she was a second self.

Since Dave had assured her she was dead ringer for the real Nancy, they hadn't worried about changing superficial behaviors like her gestures or her clothing or her voice. Kelly doubted she could have memorized the events in Nancy's life and endless facts about the Summerhill family history and tried to alter her behavior at the same time. It would have been too much to expect and she was glad she didn't have to do it.

For his part, as time went on, Dave became more and more astounded at Kelly's progress toward being Nancy and more and more anxious as to whether or not it was time to put their work to the test. He himself, having come to know her, could see where and how she differed from Nancy in temperament and attitude, where she was uniquely Kelly.

Yet he was also startled by the naturalness with which Kelly portrayed Nancy, and the apparent ease with which she absorbed and incorporated the stories he related of Nancy's experiences and Nancy's actions.

Half of the time, he couldn't believe Kelly was *not* Nancy—

even though he knew better—and in the course of teaching her everything he could remember about Nancy, he would be startled to realize she had never previously heard whatever story he was relating. He guessed his sense of dislocation was akin to what it must feel like to tell a past event to an amnesiac who had experienced the event but could no longer recall it.

The biggest problem, though, was not whether he could believe she was Nancy, but whether her father and her brother could believe it. The problem of introducing her to them in such a way that they would accept her as the genuine article gnawed at him continually.

It wasn't so much the 'how' or even the explanations he and Kelly had devised and planned to present for her disappearance and re-appearance that he worried over, but those things that reside below consciousness: those gut sensations, pheromones, intuitions and hidden knowings that her father and brother might have about Nancy that Dave, despite his closeness to the family, might know nothing about.

He woke up many nights in a sweat, wondering what he didn't know that would one day trip Kelly up, once she had been accepted into the Summerhill clan. What, his mind frequently accused him, was he *not* preparing her for?

Summer was moving into Indian Summer, a gorgeously serene time of the year in New Mexico. The air was not as hot, the nights were cooler, the wind was non-existent. The color of the light was crystalline and shimmering, and the very air radiated stillness.

The perfection of the fall weather had ignited Kelly with a new ambition: oil painting. At her behest, Dave had bought her the art materials she needed to get started and, one Saturday, as he dried the dishes from their lunch, he watched her through the kitchen window as she paced back and forth in front of her new easel, which had been set up in the backyard. She was painting a still life of gold and red apples she had arranged on the picnic table.

At first he had thought the painting would distract her from the hard task of learning all there was to know about Nancy but instead, he saw that it had relaxed her and allowed her to absorb even more information. The right side of her brain, he supposed, needed a different kind of creative task to balance all of the exercise he was giving to the verbal left side.

Dave pulled a beer from the refrigerator and went out to sit on the back porch. If he had been straight, he realized, he would be quite interested in Kelly. He loved her vigor and her dogged persistence about every task she undertook.

He respected the fact that once she had agreed to his crazy scheme, she had gone after it wholeheartedly. He didn't know what her own motives might be in the matter—other than the enticement of the foundry—but he had been afraid to question them too closely.

He didn't want to scare her off, particularly at this late stage of the learning game, but he wondered at what point *he* had gotten so invested in the success of their venture. Was it really all for a smile from Jim as he had told Kelly? Or was there something else at stake for him? If there was, he didn't consciously know what it might be.

Dave took a sip of his beer and studied Kelly's emerging still life. The apples were a bit lopsided and the shading wasn't quite right but he thought it wasn't bad for a beginner. Kelly actually had quite a lot of artistic talent.

She had never done any bronze casting but he had already made her memorize every step in the foundry process, the floor plan of Summerhill foundry, the accounting and marketing end of the business, and the names and finished works of every major and minor Summerhill past customer.

Because he didn't dare risk taking her to Santa Fe museums or galleries, he had brought photos of the multitudes of small fine art works that had been cast at Summerhill and information about the works' present location.

He had even made her memorize the names and locations and ownership of every major Santa Fe, Dallas and Phoenix art gallery that had any contact with the Summerhill family. She had had to memorize the names, faces and bios of every significant Summerhill family friend, artist, and tradesman contact.

Already, she knew five times as much about the business as Walter knew. But then again, if she didn't, how was she ever going to convince Jim she was her father's daughter? Even though the truth was, she wasn't?

"What do you think?" Kelly stepped away from her easel, her *Girls Rule* bill cap sitting rakishly on her head.

"Not bad for a beginner."

"Jeez!"

"Just teasing," Dave assured, "It's coming along nicely. Take a break from the sun. I'll get you a beer."

He brought out a Corona and handed it to her where she sat sprawled in the shade of the porch, eyeing her newest creation. Her potter's wheel was also set up in the backyard, the grass around it beaten down with use.

"The shadowing isn't right."

"No."

"Shadowing is difficult."

"Shadowing is what makes the final result mellow or bright or jarring or pleasing. Shadowing—"

"—leads the viewer to experience what you want them to experience."

"Shadowing creates the depth that makes illusion real."

They both knew they weren't talking about the painting anymore.

"Are you feeling ready?" Dave asked in a small quiet voice.

"I don't know," Kelly shrugged. "Do I have anything else to learn?"

"Nothing that I'm consciously aware of."

The answer left them both equally unsatisfied, equally restless.

"Maybe we're just afraid of taking the plunge," Kelly twirled the beer bottle between her palms.

"Do you have cold feet?" Dave sat forward in his chair.

"Some."

"Are you backing out?"

"No."

"Kelly, there is one final thing."

"What is it?"

"It could be a deal breaker."

Kelly's eyes went wide. She had grown to trust Dave, even like him, and she didn't want to get bad news now. Her faith in him, in this scheme, was tenuous at times. But over the course of the summer it had strengthened. "Is there something you haven't told me, Dave?"

"Your father, Jim—"

Kelly had grown adjusted to thinking of Jim Summerhill as her father and Walter Summerhill as her brother so Dave's choice of phrase no longer jarred her.

"—was never very happy about Nancy's—your—being gay."

"What are you saying? He knew about it and didn't like it? She never told him? She told him and they had a big blowout? What?"

"She never got a chance to tell him. She told me and then up and vanished the next week. I had advised her to wait to tell him, to have her fling with Barbara and be sure, absolutely sure of her sexuality before she told him."

"He could hardly have been homophobic. I mean he accepted you. Why did you tell her to wait?"

"I'm not his son, Kelly. It wouldn't have been quite the same thing to learn that his daughter was gay."

"If she never talked to him about it, how do you know he was unhappy about it?"

"It was what he told me later, years after she was gone."

"What did he tell you?"

Dave looked flustered. "I warned you he was a traditionalist."

"Spill it, Dave." Kelly was beginning to feel agitated. Sweat had risen under the collar of her light cotton t-shirt.

"All right. He believes a woman needs a man to survive in our misogynist world. He doesn't think lesbian sex is unnatural, he just thinks it's meaningless."

Kelly snorted. "Meaningless?"

Dave shrugged. "Just not important, Kelly. In other words, fine as a sideline, but nothing any right-thinking woman would commit herself to. Women need men to be whole. That would be the way Jim would think of it."

"And to think I was beginning to like the old bastard."

"Kelly," Dave leaned over to touch her on the knee. She brushed off his touch, jumped up, and started to pace.

"What the hell do you want me to do? You aren't asking me to hide my queerness, are you?"

Dave looked down, his knuckles white where he grasped the empty beer bottle. He nodded, then looked up.

"It might be for the best, Kelly."

"Hell, no!"

"At least until he got used to you. Until he adjusted to having you around. Until—"

"Until what? Until he rewrote the will? What the hell are you thinking, Dave?"

"I'm just asking you to give him some time."

"What about me and Barbara?"

"You could tell him it was a fling and you've...reformed." Dave's head drooped.

"Reformed?" She snorted again and then she shouted, the veins at her temples visibly pulsing. "You, of all people, should know it's impossible to *reform*. Besides, it wasn't a fling!"

"Kelly," he said quietly, "it didn't happen to you."

"To carry this thing off, I have to believe that it did." She shook her head in frustrated anger and threw the empty beer bottle at the table, scattering the apples in all directions. "I can't believe you've left this for last, Dave."

"I'm sorry, Kelly. But it's the hardest thing of all to talk about."

Her hands were balled into clenched fists. He hated to face her at such a moment. Still, he had to know her answer. "Is it a deal breaker?"

"I don't know, Dave. I have to think about it." She strode into the house, slamming the screen door behind her. Dave tossed his own beer bottle at the few remaining apples and then dropped his head into his hands.

Eleven a.m. on September 15th was the time and day they

FOUR

chose for Kelly to make her appearance at the foundry. It was the second Tuesday of the month and Dave would be holding his regular monthly meeting with Jim to review the foundry accounts. Walter was scheduled to compete in a catamaran race on Cochiti Lake and Alice would be grocery shopping.

Rose, the foundry manager, would be in a design meeting with an important client. The foundry's other two employees, Atavema Griego of Cochiti Pueblo and Jeff Wiley, would be in the foundry working on projects in various stages of completion. Atavema would remember the teenage Nancy, but Rose and Jeff had both come on board since Nancy's disappearance.

Dave thought it best if Kelly had to deal only with the old man to start with. She could meet the others later. Later, when Jim was over some of the shock and—they hoped—had been partially won over.

Dave, for his part, would, of course, act flabbergasted and

then suspicious—as befitted an accountant—and demand proof of her identity. Kelly knew exactly what proof he would demand and how she would answer. They had rehearsed every question and answer a hundred times, as if they were preparing for an elaborate and complex and—in the end, unpredictable—stage play.

Kelly had packed all of her worldly goods into her truck, including her new painting equipment, the evening before. In the morning, she showered for the last time at Dave's apartment and put on a simple pink oxford shirt and blue jeans. She pulled out of Dave's driveway at 9 a.m., giving herself two hours—double the required amount of time—to get to Santa Fe.

She drove slowly, breathing deeply, sipping bottled water, and forcing herself to admire the multi-toned desert landscape for the sixty mile drive. When she got to the outskirts of town, she took the Cerrillos Road exit as Dave had instructed. The route took her past dying motels and gas stations and when she reached the road leading to the airport, she turned west, her heart starting to pound in her chest.

She checked her pocket watch: 10:46. She drove even more slowly down the four-lane roadway, which Dave told her had been a two-lane when Nancy disappeared. There were a half-dozen new business along the strip of the road and Dave had taught her which she should pretend to recognize and which should appear new to her.

Kelly sucked in a breath, beginning to feel real fear. What if she forgot everything? What if the moment she saw Jim Summerhill in his wheelchair—something that had happened after Nancy disappeared, which meant her initial reaction to the old man had to be natural trepidation followed by sheer horror—what if, all she wanted to do was turn and run?

Coming up on the left, Kelly saw for the first time the proud uprights of angle iron encasing the welded sign that announced *Summerhill Foundry, Fine Arts Casting*. The pounding of her heart in her ears drowned out the sound of her truck downshifting.

She drove on down the asphalt of the roadway, past the entrance, her feet unwilling to tap the brakes, her arms too uncoordinated to turn the wheel. It wasn't that every fiber in her being said *No! Don't go in there!*, it was instead that every fiber of her being said, *Yes. This is home.* It was inexplicable, but something in that unassuming angle iron sign called to her.

Kelly pulled over to the side of the road, waited for the traffic to ease and then made a u-turn. She checked her watch again. 10:54. Six minutes.

Kelly pulled into the gravel-packed yard of the foundry and parked her truck in exactly the space that had been Nancy's. She knew which one it was because Dave had described it to her.

Parked next to her was Dave's oversized black 4-wheel drive, Atavema's pert blue Chevy Corsica, Jeff's red Toyota pickup and the full-size tan Ford pickup truck belonging to Rose's design customer. There were no other vehicles in evidence and no one walking around the grounds.

Kelly breathed a sign of relief. So far so good. She turned off her truck's engine and glanced at the buildings, absorbing in three dimensions what she already knew from the two dimensions of Dave's maps and elevations.

The single story , brown stucco building directly in front of her was the foundry office, which included a reception area with a high counter, Jim's office, a conference room, and the hallway that led to Jim's private residence—the house Nancy had grown up in—which Jim now shared with Alice.

Blindfolded, and with Dave leading her around a full-scale 'map' he had staked out on the grass in the backyard, she had learned the location of everything in the building, even wall hangings.

It had taken Dave weeks to piece together which furnishings and paintings and art pieces were new since Nancy's disappearance and, therefore, which ones she would need to express surprise over. She also had to know those with which she would be comfortably familiar, and which, she—as Nancy—had held opinions about.

Kelly knew Alice existed but as she had come into Jim's life after Nancy disappeared, she and Dave had decided it would be best for Dave to tell her nothing about the woman so she could form her own natural reaction to her.

Off to Kelly's right was the foundry itself: a two-story hip-roofed building framed with steel beams and covered in sheet metal siding in a faded yellow. At its entrance, a triangle of blue gamma grass acted as a display park for three small-scale bronze sculptures. Two of them were post-Nancy. Dave had described them in detail to her and sketched crude drawings of each.

Off to Kelly's left was a squat 4-bedroom, 2-bath brown stucco modular home that had been set down on concrete footings a number of years after Nancy's disappearance. The bedrooms had been converted into Rose's and Walter's offices and living quarters for Rose. The remaining bedroom was used as storage. Walter lived in an apartment several miles down Airport Road.

Dave had told her that Walter drove a restored 1962 cherry red Mustang and a fairly new Dodge Ram pickup, neither of which had been in his possession at the time of Nancy's disappearance. Walter had been driving a souped-up apple-green Buick Skylark in those days that, junked and rotting, was still parked behind Jim's house. He'd also possessed a grey open-air Jeep with a rollbar.

10:59. Kelly got out of her truck, slamming the truck door, which resounded in the Tuesday morning quiet. Her knees wobbled, but her steps and her lines were well-rehearsed.

All she had to do was walk in through the front door, circle behind the counter, go down the short hallway and stop within the open door of the first room on her left. Dave would have his back to the door and Jim Summerhill would be looking straight at her. Once he saw her, she only had to utter one word.

As if in a dream, Kelly carried out the actions. Stepping across the final threshold into Jim Summerhill's office, she entered a world where the ephemera of another woman's ghost lingered. She hadn't expected it, but it didn't surprise her either. Kelly felt the ghost rush toward her but she could do nothing to resist it. The ghost recognized her and knew why she had come.

She heard the ghost's secret cry of victory and then felt it suffuse the fresh emptiness of her lungs and rise like a soft exhaled mist into her mind. It wasn't painful or frightening. It was inevitable. She was truly Nancy now.

Other than the ghost, which had been subsumed into Kelly in a moment that existed outside of time and which neither of the men could have perceived, Kelly Bransford saw nothing in the room Dave Paxton had helped her to memorize except Jim Summerhill's pained old blue eyes lifting to meet hers.

"Dad," she said.

"Nancy!" The old man's eyes were wide, his mouth agape.

FIVE

Dave Paxton jumped from his chair, his eyes just as wide, but his jaw tight. "Who in the hell are you?"

"Dave," she turned toward him, her shaking hands the only sign of her fright. "Dave, you remember me. I'm Nancy."

"Nancy's dead!"

"Dave!" Jim Summerhill was breathing heavily as he shouted. "It's Nancy! Nancy's come back!"

"Jim! How could it be Nancy? Nancy's—"

"—dead." Kelly answered. "We heard you. But I'm not dead, Dave. I'm right here. Look," she held out her arms, "flesh and blood."

"Well, then," Dave roared, " where in the hell have you been? Do you have any idea how much suffering you've caused your father?"

Kelly was slowly approaching Jim Summerhill. "Dad," she said softly, leaning over him, "what happened?"

"Car wreck, honey. About four years ago."

"God," Kelly started to cry, "how are you getting around? Who's taking care of you?"

Jim Summerhill's eyes brimmed with tears. "Dave here. Alice."

"Alice?"

"My...wife, honey. She's...you'll like her. You'll like her a lot, Nancy."

"Jim," Dave moved between them. "You don't even know who in the hell this is!" He turned to Kelly. "Can I see some kind of identification, Ms. Whoever-You-Are?"

"Jeez, Dave," Kelly dug into her jeans for her wallet, "What are you so damn surly about? Not meeting any cute guys these days or what?"

Dave Paxton stopped dead, his body rigid with feigned surprise.

"I assume," Nancy went on, "that you haven't changed your ways. Haven't abandoned 'the life' and settled down with a nice little woman, now have you?"

Jim Summerhill grinned. "He hasn't changed a damn thing, except that he frets over me endlessly."

Kelly smiled at Jim.

"Christ!" Dave exploded at both of them, snatching the Colorado driver's license from Kelly's hand. It was one he had had a friend manufacture for him. It would not have passed official inspection, but it would probably meet Jim Summerhill's review, particularly as he hadn't even gotten to the suspicious stage.

And why hadn't he? Dave wondered. *Were they carrying off that perfect of an acting job or was the old man so desperate to have his daughter resurrected that he would have believed anything?*

Dave held out the license for Jim's inspection. "Summerhill, huh?" He ruminated, glancing at the name. "So you haven't gotten married."

"No, Dad. I haven't gotten married."

There was a long silence while Jim Summerhill struggled visibly with his emotions. He swallowed convulsively a few times and then his voice, when he found it, was hardly above a whisper. "Where have you been, baby?"

Kelly knelt beside the wheelchair and took Jim's dry featherweight hand in her own. "It's a long story, Daddy."

"You didn't call...or write." Jim's voice was still a whisper and his eyes filled with fresh tears that brimmed over and rolled down his defenseless cheeks.

"I was afraid." Kelly wiped away the tears with her fingers. Dave Paxton stood staring down at them, floored by Kelly's acting ability. If he hadn't rationally known she wasn't Nancy, he would have sworn in a court of law without an iota of doubt that she was Jim Summerhill's daughter, returned from the dead.

"Afraid of what?"

"Afraid you couldn't accept me for being with Barbara and running away with her and..."

"I'm not an ogre."

"I know. It's just the longer I was away, the harder it became to call you and we didn't have any money and it was hard to get from day to day and..."

"Where's Barbara now?"

"She left me high and dry at a truck stop in South Dakota about ten months after we ran away. She hitched a ride on a semi going east and I never heard from her again. I hoofed around and found odd jobs and was just too embarrassed to come home, Dad. I didn't have anything to show for myself."

"Oh, baby," he said.

Kelly stood up. "And I'm not expecting anything now, Dad. I just wanted to ask you for a job. If you don't have one, I'll just head on out again. You don't owe me anything. It's just that I've done a lot of potting, Dad," Kelly wiped away a tear of her own, "but I miss casting so much and I had some ideas for a few pieces and I was just praying that maybe..."

Jim Summerhill started to cry in earnest. Dave glanced at Kelly in astonishment and then grabbed tissues from the box on the desk and held one to the old man's nose while he blew it. Through tears, he took another look at his daughter. "You cut your long beautiful hair," he softly accused.

"It was too much trouble to take care of on the road, Dad."

"That cut looks good, actually. Perky. Strong. I'm glad you didn't pierce your nose or your lip or something."

Dave laughed and Kelly grinned, "It wouldn't go with the dominant Summerhill chin, Dad."

Jim Summerhill smiled, his eyes bright with astonishment. He looked at Dave Paxton. "She really is my daughter. Is there space in the modular?"

"Uh...well, there's the extra bedroom. It's got a bunch of stuff stored in it but, uh..."

"Get it cleaned out. Do you have a lot of stuff, Nancy?"

Kelly shook her head. "Just my truck and my fired pieces and some tools and supplies. A couple of changes of clothes. That's it."

"Sounds like a Summerhill to me, Dave. Traveling light."

Kelly grinned. Dave laid his head on one side, his face perplexed. "This is just too weird."

"What do you mean, Dave?" Kelly asked.

"Lost people don't just pop up seven years later in the middle of an autumn morning. Lost people don't just come back from the...ah, never mind."

Jim Summerhill smiled, dismissing Dave's fears. "You two get that room cleaned out and get Nancy moved in."

Dave shook his head, his eyes troubled. "Whatever you say, Jim. You're the boss."

"And then get back here for lunch. I'll want you to meet Alice, Nancy."

"Of course, Dad." She gestured toward the door with her hand and looked at Dave. "After you, Dave."

They had nearly finished emptying Kelly's new bedroom of artists' drawings, boxes of old invoices, and miscellaneous sports equipment (some belonging to Rose and some belonging to Walter) when Rose Twill came into the modular, the screen door slamming behind her.

"Dave?"

"Back here," he called.

"I saw your truck out—" She came into the bedroom and her eyes widened at the sight of the now nearly empty space.

"What's going on in here, Dave, and who the hell is that?"

Kelly stopped trying to lift a sizeable box and stood up. "I'm Nancy Summerhill." She reached out a hand to shake Rose's hand, very aware that her heart was doing a hot little tattoo in her throat because Rose Twill was utterly gorgeous.

The young woman was dressed in a faded denim shirt which was unbuttoned low enough to show off the tan trench of deep cleavage between full and shapely breasts, and dark blue jeans that hugged her trim hips and slim thighs. She was a head taller than Nancy and her hair was a short bouncy mass of dark curls. Her face was heart-shaped and she had dark lashes outlining warm hazel eyes.

"Who?" Rose's full lips formed a perfect sexy round and Kelly felt a breathless heat suffuse her chest. Rose reached out automatically to accept Kelly's proffered hand.

"Jim's daughter," Dave explained as the two women shook hands, not missing Kelly's palpable excitement. *Jeez,* he thought, *how was she going to keep her bargain about suppressing her sexuality if she was living in the same bloody house as Rose?* Not that he thought Rose was gay, but he doubted that the Kelly he had gotten to know over the last few months, once set on her course, was going to take *no* for an answer from any woman, gay or straight. And he could practically sniff the female pheromones Kelly was emitting in Rose's direction.

"Jim's daughter?" repeated Rose. "But—"

"I've been gone a long time."

"No shit."

"Do you mind my sharing your house for awhile?"

"You're moving in here?" Rose's expression vacillated between disbelief and annoyance.

"If it's a problem—"

"Well, it's just...it's kind of tight in here already. I don't know how we're all going to fit. I mean Walter's here during the day sometimes and I'm in and out and..."

"I can make this one room my living quarters and my office, both. I don't need much space."

Rose shrugged. "Whatever. I mean—" she glared at Dave, "I obviously didn't have any say in this anyway." Rose turned and stamped out of the room.

Kelly looked imploringly at Dave, who rolled his eyes. "All right, I'll try to make amends with her but obviously it's going to take some adjusting."

Kelly responded in a low voice, in case Rose was still within earshot. "We didn't really expect Jim to just move me right in."

"No, we didn't."

"But I hate to get off on the wrong foot with her. Everything is going to be difficult enough as it is."

"Yeah," he whispered, "particularly with the eyes you're making at her. Knock it off, okay?"

"Dave," Kelly whispered back, "screw you."

"You promised."

"You didn't tell me she was gorgeous! And that I'd be rooming with her!"

"It didn't occur to me. Besides I think—"

"What?"

"I think she and your brother Walter might be...doing it."

"Oh, Lord," It was Kelly's turn to roll her eyes, "I think I've moved to Peyton Place."

"You probably have. I'll go talk to her."

Dave thought he had never seen Jim Summerhill so keyed up. At least, not so keyed up since the accident that had taken away his mobility. Not that Jim could suddenly miraculously move but the look of excitement in his eyes was palpable.

That intensity, that joy in living and doing reminded Dave of the Jim he had known before the accident: the man who would rise with great energy in the middle of the night to draw or mold a figure because it had come into his head in his sleep.

Jim's wheelchair was drawn up to the sturdy dining table in the bright country kitchen which had been entirely redecorated in bold reds and sunny yellows by Alice. Kelly stopped short when she saw it.

"Wow!" she exclaimed. "This is a sea change!"

"Do you like it?" Jim asked.

"Yes," she smiled at the man in the wheelchair, "it's much more cheerful, Dad." Kelly had been told the prior kitchen had been a rather drab and uninspired combo of tans and greens.

Standing with her back to them facing the stove was a slight narrow-shouldered woman. "Soup's on," the woman remarked, turning and casually handing Kelly a soup bowl. Kelly swallowed hard and accepted it. "I'm Nancy," she said, by way of explanation.

"I know who you are," the woman replied matter-of-factly. "I'm Alice. Just sit yourself down with that bowl. Crackers and spoons are on the table."

"Thank you," Kelly replied. She was very careful to go to the place at the table that had been Nancy's. When she settled the bowl of soup on the table in front of Nancy's chair, she was startled by a gasp from Jim Summerhill. Kelly's head shot up in alarm. "Are you okay?"

Jim's eyes had filled with tears again. "Oh, my god," he moaned, "you really are Nancy." The old man's chest heaved as he tried to get a breath between tears. "Oh, my god."

Dave was standing over Jim, almost cooing to him. "Jim, it's okay. It's okay."

"Dave," Jim croaked, "I never expected to feel this happy again. Not ever." Tears streamed down his lined cheeks. Dave stroked them away with his thumbs, his own eyes filling with tears.

"Jim, Jim."

"Just let me cry, Dave. Let me cry. These are tears of unspeakable joy."

"You crazy old man," Dave whispered.

"My daughter's come home, Dave. I still can't move, but my life is restored. I have a new life!"

"Yes, Jim, you do. I know, too, that your daughter has truly come home and that she's going to do everything in her power to live up to your every expectation." Dave looked across the table at Kelly, his face somber with silent warning.

Kelly looked back, comprehending for the first time in a visceral way how deeply invested Dave was in this charade...and how much was at stake. To Dave, it really wasn't about the foundry or the money, just as he'd said. It was about love...about love for the man who had taken him in and offered him healing.

It meant, if Kelly failed, she would not be breaking a verbal agreement. She would be committing an act of betrayal because to break the bond between lover and beloved, even if that love was not sexual, was to betray. Betrayal was a sin that was never forgiven.

Dave was telling her, with a single look, that her imposture was no longer a game, if it ever had been. She was in for keeps.

After lunch, Dave and Kelly walked across the graveled park-

SIX

ing lot to the foundry. Kelly was breathing deeply and focusing, trying to remember everything Dave had told her about the foundry. About what would appear to be new to her and what would not.

Jim's motor-powered wheelchair rode smoothly along on the guard-railed plywood ramp that had been built for him which extended the full distance from the house to the foundry entrance.

The foundry was rectangular in shape and arranged in the order of the steps involved in lost wax casting, beginning to the left of the entrance and circling around the inside of the building with one main wide central aisle.

Pony walls divided the sections from each other, except for the ceramic molding, kiln-firing and pouring areas which were enclosed together along the back and right side of the building by a full concrete block wall. Both the kiln for firing the clay and the furnace for heating the bronze were noisy and hot and better separated from the other steps in the process.

"So, Dad," Kelly commented once they were inside, "it looks like we're still casting mostly small pieces." She was gazing at the wall-mounted plywood counter circling the first section of the foundry which was littered with clay works in various stages of completion. The sign mounted on the wall said: Clay Reduction and Enlarging. In this stage of the process, artists who had commissioned the foundry to cast their piece worked with Atavema or Rose to create either an enlarged or reduced clay model of their original work.

"Right," he agreed. "We could pour in sections and weld the pieces together. We have the equipment as you know. Walter just hasn't been able to attract the business. Rose worked with Stacy Allcraft on one large piece—it was a full-size male nude—which was quite a success. I'd like to see more of that."

They moved on to the next section, titled Molding, and here Kelly exclaimed, "Dad, where's the plaster of paris?"

"What you're seeing here," his own excitement was palpable, "is one of the biggest advances in casting, Nancy! No more plaster molds. We use a silicone rubber mold now to form a negative mold from the positive clay model."

"Wow," Kelly rubbed her hands together. "I can hardly wait to get started!" They ambled up to the next section, titled Wax Positive, which struck Kelly more as an admonition to be happy than a phase in the casting process.

Here, sitting on plywood counters were seven reddish brown figures. Some were abstracts, some were finely detailed human busts and heads, some were animals. They looked exactly like clay figures except that each was a hollow wax casting and had been formed by rotating the negative silicone mold while hot wax was poured into it which coated the mold with a precise thickness of wax. Once the wax cooled, the silicone mold was peeled away from it, leaving the wax positive.

Kelly was feeling a little nervous as they approached the concrete wall that separated the ceramic mold baths from the wax positive section because one of the people who would remember the real Nancy was behind that wall.

Dave had told her that Atavema Griego was a Native American woman with four children and six grandchildren who drove herself daily to the foundry from Cochiti Pueblo, about 25 miles to the south. The molding half of the foundry was her domain which she shared only with Rose and the commissioning artists themselves, having little use for Walter. Dave was of the belief that Atavema had had a soft spot for the teenage Nancy, treating her as she would one of her own children, but he could not predict her reaction to Nancy's return.

When they entered the Ceramic Mold section, Atavema had her back to them because she was dipping and turning a table-sized wax positive of a rearing horse in a bath of what was essentially a slurry of liquefied stucco. Drying ceramic molds stood on shelves around them. "Atavema," Kelly called, her voice anxious.

Atavema turned and Kelly saw the woman's round face for the first time. She had a sweet mothering smile and the moment she saw Kelly, her face broke out into a grin. "So," she said in the style of understatement common to many Native Americans, "you came back, huh?"

Kelly grinned, liking the woman immediately. "Yes, I did."

"Good," Atavema said, stretching her back, even while holding aloft the dripping piece she was in the process of coating in her gloved hands. She was a solid, big breasted woman with an air of quiet centered calm and, Kelly guessed, a devilish sense of humor. "We need you. Maybe your dad will put you right to work." She winked at Jim Summerhill in his wheelchair and he grinned back.

"Tomorrow," Kelly assured her. "I start tomorrow."

Atavema laughed softly and Kelly knew the interview with her was over. She didn't know if she had passed muster, but she assumed she had. Dave patted her on the shoulder and she turned her eyes to view what most people assumed a foundry to be, namely that place in which solid metal becomes liquid and is transformed into works of art: the Kiln and the Furnace. Her first sight of it gave Kelly a flutter of unbearable excitement in her stomach.

In the kiln, the wax positive mold—which was now held prisoner inside the body of the ceramic mold—was heated until the wax drained out, giving the process its name, 'lost wax'. The ceramic mold was then baked to harden it to accept the melted bronze. The melted bronze would be poured into the baked ceramic mold resulting in the essential bronze casting.

Rose, wearing elbow-high fireproof gloves, was tending to the furnace, in which bars of bronze alloy were melting, and she looked murderously at Dave and not at all at Kelly or Jim. With the furnace blasting, it was too noisy to talk and it was hot, despite the fact that much of the wall between the kiln and the furnace consisted of a chain operated double-wide metal door that had been rolled open, allowing the cooler outside air to circulate into the building.

Kelly thought Rose was even more gorgeous with bronze slag marring her forehead and sweat rolling down her neck, dampening the cloth of her shirt between her high breasts.

"When do you pour today?" Dave shouted over the din of the furnace.

"In about an hour," Rose shouted back.

"Jeff usually helps her," Dave said into Kelly's ear. "If he's not here, Walter helps. It's about the only damn thing we can get him to do."

"Pouring is exciting," Kelly pointed out, as they walked away.

"Yeah, I think that's why Walter will do it. The rest of it just doesn't interest him. Too tedious, I guess."

They had moved on to the Devestment section of the foundry where the ceramic molds were broken away from the cooled bronze casting using hammers and pneumatic drills. Once the bronze was revealed, it was sandblasted and then sent to the Metal Work section where it was welded, if necessary, and the welding seams chased.

Lastly, it went to Patina where it was given its final finish by the brushing or spraying on of chemicals that oxidized with the metal to achieve intended colors and surface effects. Jeff Wiley was king of these three post-pouring sections of the foundry.

He was a tall, thin man with intensely blue eyes, spiked hair the color of corn, and the remote air of the solitary, deeply dedicated craftsman. He was chasing seams from the back leg of a hand-sized bronze of a dog curled in sleep. At the sight of Jim and Dave and Kelly, he politely turned off his sander and removed his mask and gloves. When Kelly was introduced as Nancy, he shook her hand and welcomed her aboard. The moment she turned away, he re-vested and went back to his work.

A moment later, they were outside again. "So, pumpkin," Jim said, "what do you think?"

"I think I'm ready to get to work!"

Jim Summerhill laughed. "Tomorrow. You get settled in. I'll expect you in the office at 9 a.m. sharp. Don't disappoint me."

"I won't," Kelly answered.

"Good." Jim's chin pressed the control on his wheelchair and he motored away.

"Whew," she sighed, when he was out of earshot. "How did I do?"

"Perfect. Get some rest because you're going to need it. I'll see you tomorrow. So far, so good."

"Does he believe us?"

"I don't know. But he sure as hell wants to."

There were two hours of September daylight still remaining on her first day at Summerhill Foundry but Kelly was exhausted. She finished stacking boxes of fired and unfired clay figures in her new room. Then she lay flat on the unaccustomed softness of the bed, too tired to move her body, even while her overwrought brain churned out thoughts with relentless intensity.

Supper had not been discussed and she had not dared to ask about it. She had learned that Walter was not expected back at the foundry until the following morning and she assumed that would be when she met him. He was another hurdle to clear. A very high hurdle.

She had been raised as an only child by her adoptive parents so she wasn't sure how a person behaved with a brother. He would probably be far more suspicious of her than Jim and might have some way to detect that she wasn't Nancy. Some way Dave could not know about.

Jim, she had realized as the day wore on, had a stake in her being Nancy. He wanted her to be Nancy and might not be inclined to look a gift horse in the mouth. Walter, on the other hand, was sure to have a stake in her *not* being Nancy, since it might threaten his inheritance. Kelly's head spun and her empty stomach growled its hunger.

Slowly, she sat up and forced her stiffening body off the bed. She headed down the hallway and into the small practical kitchen. There was a plain white refrigerator, a microwave, an aluminum-framed window over the single porcelain sink and cheap birch-veneered wood cabinets.

The floor was covered in linoleum of an indeterminate tan color and the counter top was a slightly-darker speckled tan Formica. It was uninspired but not awful and it was clean. Clearly, Rose ran a tight ship in her office/home.

Rose, cleaned up from her day and wearing jeans and a T-shirt screen printed with a bright red and blue advertisement for the All-Indian Rodeo in Window Rock, Arizona was sitting at the round kitchen table, which was covered in a cheery green oilcloth, munching on a sandwich and flipping through an art magazine. Kelly automatically opened the refrigerator door and peered inside.

"You didn't buy anything in there," Rose growled, "so don't touch anything."

Kelly straightened up and turned to face her. "I guess we need to make some rules."

"The rules are simple," Rose said, not glancing up from her magazine, "you stay away from me and I'll stay away from you."

"I don't think it's going to be that simple," Kelly said, wondering at the animosity. Hadn't Dave talked to Rose, like he said he would?

"Why not?" Rose shot back.

"Well, we're in the same space. Are you suggesting I buy a refrigerator and a microwave? And what about the bathroom?"

"Yeah, well," Rose's fingers gripped her sandwich so hard they were compressing the soft bread into a thin sheet, "you're the big boss lady now so you just go ahead and make up whatever the hell rules you want. I was told to cooperate."

Kelly felt herself nearing a flashpoint. The day had drained her of every last ounce of diplomacy she was capable of mustering. She slammed shut the refrigerator door and dashed down the hallway to her room. The moment she reached her bed, she threw herself face down on it and burst into tears.

Rationally, she knew her tears were an expression of too many emotions experienced in one day: shock, elation, exhaustion, and fear. She didn't know what was going to come next and she had hoped, if nothing else, to get along with Rose. If Rose and Walter both stalemated her, she was going to be in for a long hard struggle.

And why shouldn't they? She was an interloper, no matter what provenance she claimed, no matter what story Jim swallowed. Rose and Walter could make her life hell. And they probably would.

"I'm sorry." There was a soft voice at the door. Kelly twisted her head and saw Rose standing in the doorway, her arms crossed over her chest. Kelly sat up and wiped at her tears in embarrassment.

"I'm sorry," Kelly mumbled. "It's been a long day. I'll do everything I can to stay out of your way."

"I...I was just pissed off, that's all. I mean nobody told me anything. I didn't know you were coming, and...that you were going to move in, and..."

"Nobody knew I was coming. I wasn't expecting anything from anyone. I just wanted to let my...dad...know I was alive...after all these years."

"Why did you come back?"

"I don't know. Why does anyone come back? Maybe we're just homing pigeons at heart." Her voice was disparaging.

For the first time, Rose laughed. The sound made Kelly's heart lighten and her fingers tingle.

"That's funny," Rose said. "Have you had any dinner?"

"No."

"C'mon. I'll take you out for a burrito. Just to show you there's no hard feelings."

They went in Rose's pickup truck, an aging sky blue Toyota with a full camper shell attached. "It costs me more in gas," Rose said, referring to the aerodynamic drag created by the camper, "but I like to sneak away sometimes."

"Where do you go?"

"Oh, everywhere. New Mexico's full of great back country...whoops, sorry. You already know that."

Kelly nodded, but knew she was faking. She hardly knew anything about New Mexico's out-of-doors. Dave had mentioned Cochiti Lake and Bandelier National Monument as places Nancy's family had gone in her childhood but she didn't know anything about them except where they were located on the map.

"Do you hike or what?"

"Hike, rock climb, canoe."

"I like to hike, too."

They pulled into a strip mall that was less than half a mile from the foundry and went into a storefront eatery where all of the signs were handwritten in Spanish with colored markers.

"*Sabes que quieren?*" A young woman came out of a curtained doorway and paused at the cash register.

"*Quiero un burrito con carne, por favor,*" Rose answered. She turned to Kelly. "Do you know what you want?"

"Why don't you make it two?"

Rose turned back to the cashier and held up two fingers.

"*Dos*."

The woman took their drink order and then rang up the ticket, which Rose paid. They accepted their drinks and headed over to sit at a small grungy table. Rose took a sip of her soda.

"We've had a lot of Mexican nationals move into this part of Santa Fe in the last few years. The long-term resident Hispanic population kind of looks down on them."

"Why?"

"They work for low wages and wire their money home to their families in Mexico."

"It's a big change," Kelly agreed. "I don't remember any of these businesses. This strip mall wasn't even here." She wasn't up on the state of local politics—although she'd forced herself to read the daily newspaper at Dave's house to get a sense of New Mexican concerns—but she knew from Dave's coaching that the strip mall was new since Nancy's time.

"How long ago did you leave?" Rose asked.

"It was seven years ago." Kelly scrunched her shoulders down and fiddled with her straw. She hated to lie to Rose. It was much harder than lying to Jim because she had been prepared to lie to Jim.

"Why did you leave?"

Kelly shrugged. "Young and dumb, I guess. Impulsive."

"I heard you didn't run away alone."

"That's true. Barbara..."

"Whose idea was it?"

Kelly swallowed. She had practiced this story but she hadn't given deep thought to the underlying motivations because the events hadn't happened to her. She scrunched a little further down in her seat. "It just happened, you know. I don't remember who mentioned it first."

"Were you real close friends?"

Kelly nodded and jabbed her straw around in her drink. "We were lovers."

Rose's face went white. Kelly's head shot up in surprise. "Jeez. I thought everyone knew that...I thought my dad..."

"Umm—" Rose's eyes were wide with something that looked like fear.

"*Numero quatro.*" The cashier called their order.

"That's us." Rose jumped up from her seat. Kelly followed her. They didn't speak as they grabbed their chile-smothered plates and selected plastic cutlery and rectangular packets of condiments. When they were seated again, Kelly said, "Look, you're not homophobic, are you?"

"Uh, no." Rose shook her head. "It's just...Lord, this is complicated."

"What's complicated? Dave told me you're dating my brother so it isn't like I'm going to come on to you or anything like that." It was a lie and Kelly knew it, but she was baffled by the other woman's reaction and desperate to reassure her.

"I wasn't worried about that," Rose said.

"So, what's the problem?"

"There is no problem. Look, let's just forget it, okay?"

Kelly frowned. "Okay."

Rose lifted a forkful of food to her mouth, her fingers trembling.

Shit, Kelly thought, watching her, *first she hates me, now she's terrified of me. This is going to be one miserable experience.* It wasn't as if Kelly didn't have enough complications in her life already. She went back to her original thought of the evening: she would stay as far away from Rose Twill as she could.

The next morning, Kelly got up at seven, and noticing Rose

SEVEN

was already gone, took a quick shower and got dressed. She drove two miles before locating a grocery store where she stocked up on eggs, milk, bread and cheese. She also picked up some tomatoes, lettuce, turkey sandwich meat, and canned peaches.

She figured the supplies would get her through the next few days. She didn't know what was planned and was completely in the dark about what Jim's or Walter's or Rose's regular routines might be for eating, drinking, cleaning up, talking and sleeping. She needed, as usual, to be able to take complete care of herself.

When she got back to the modular, she cleared some of Rose's items from the bottom shelf of the refrigerator and put her food away. She poured a glass of milk, toasted a piece of bread, sliced some cheese and sat down to her peasant breakfast at the table. At five minutes to nine, she walked across the parking lot to the foundry office, where she had so dramatically appeared the day before, and went in.

"Hey," Dave greeted when she got there. "How are you doing?"

"Okay."

Dave smiled at her wan expression. "Bullshit. You're wiped out."

"I know."

"It was a big day, yesterday. A very big day." Dave lowered his voice to a whisper. "But you performed perfectly. Jim bought the whole thing."

"How do you know?"

"We had a long talk last night. He's ecstatic."

Kelly sat down and raised her chin, steeling herself for a day as emotionally grueling as the preceding one. "We're not there yet, Dave. There's still Walter."

"Pshaw." Dave flapped his hand, his eyes glinting with victory. "Walter will be a piece of cake. If we play our cards right, he'll see the handwriting on the wall, take his $50,000 in cash and go find another way to support his playboy lifestyle. That's my prayer, anyway."

"What's your prayer, Dave?" Jim Summerhill was being wheeled into the room by Alice.

"My prayer is one of gratitude, Jim," Dave said without missing a beat, "that Nancy's back."

"Me, too. Oh, me too. How are you this morning, sweetheart?"

"I'm fine, Dad. How about you?"

"I doubt if I could be happier! How's the house working out? Are you getting along with Rose?"

"Everything's just perfect. You really didn't have to—"

"Nonsense," Jim interrupted. "You're my daughter. Dave's putting you on the payroll this morning. It won't be a lot at first but then I'm not going to charge you rent either."

"I'll work for free, Dad. You know that."

"You aren't working for free, Nancy Arlene Summerhill. This is your foundry, too, and you're entitled to a salary as long as you're working here. I'm paying Walter, by god, and he's not half as talented as you are."

"Speaking of Walter," Dave interrupted, "what did he say when you called him?"

"Well, of course, he was flabbergasted at first. He kept saying you were—" Jim paused, glanced nervously at Kelly, and bit his lip.

"—dead," Kelly put in, trying to ease the old man's anxiety.

"Yes. He said it over and over. I think it was just shock. But then he finally settled down and accepted the fact that you had returned."

"When is he coming over?"

"He should be here any minute."

As if summoned by a genie, Walter appeared on the threshold. He looked into the room, seeing no one but Kelly. He stared fixedly at her, his face as white as a sheet. Then he looked directly into her eyes and a moment later, a grin broke out across his features and color, as if by magic, refilled his paled cheeks. "Sis!"

Kelly stood up, baffled by the man's 180 degree turnaround. *Had she hallucinated Walter's initial reaction to her*? She glanced at Dave, whose face seemed at that very moment to be easing from a frown into a look of relief. *No,* she thought, *she hadn't imagined that moment, that moment of absolute utter terror on the part of her 'brother' because Dave had picked up on it, too.*

"So, you decided after all this time to just drop in, huh?"

Walter was moving forward to hug her and, an instant later, she found herself enveloped in his slim but well-muscled arms.

His body was stiff with tension and she felt his cool breath on her neck.

He released her—hell, practically pushed her away—after a quick squeeze and she knew intuitively the hug had been for show, for the benefit of the others, for Dave and Jim. Warning bells went off in Kelly's head, but she didn't know what they signified or what they were trying to alert her to.

Suddenly, everyone was talking at once. "You don't look a bit different," Walter said, "except for the suave haircut."

"What do you think of her?" Jim asked his son.

"I think we're all ready for that coffee break," Dave said, seeing Alice come into the room, and rising to his feet.

Dave's remark won out and Alice, without comment, wheeled Jim out of the room and the rest of them trailed after her to the kitchen. The coffee had already been brewed and a variety of pastries had been set out on the table.

Kelly was still feeling shaken when she sat down at the table. Walter sat across from her and grinned. Maybe, she thought, the man had expected to see a ghost or something. That could account for his fear. And the hug, maybe that was just the kind of person he was. Maybe he was just standoffish or insecure. Or maybe he had just never been crazy about his sister.

Kelly gave a mental shrug and decided to erase the matter from her mind. She needed all of her faculties to concentrate on talking to him and listening to him. She couldn't afford to space out.

The 'brother' sitting across from her was not unhandsome and she studied him with genuine curiosity. He was probably three inches taller than her and reasonably slim. Even so, he was not physically weak. She remembered the strength of his muscles as he had held her.

He had the distinctive dimpled Summerhill chin and the wide

high family cheekbones. His eyes were hazel like her own but with a lazy dissolute cast to them. She was sure her eyes didn't look like that. His hair was darker than hers but otherwise she could see how they could easily be assumed to be biological siblings.

"Wow," he was saying, "we were so freaked out the day you up and vanished, sis. You and Barbara."

Jim frowned. "Walter, I told you never to say that name in this house. That woman was the reason my Nancy here—"

Kelly would have sworn the glare Walter shot his father was murderous but when she looked at him, it was gone as magically as the look of fear he had given her earlier, almost as if it hadn't existed.

"Dad—" Kelly said. "I was just as much at fault."

"I don't care," Jim returned, "and I don't want to talk about it. You're here now and that's all that matters. I want to talk about the future, not the past."

"Oh, yeah, Dad," Walter put in, "what about the future?"

"The future," Jim Summerhill said, "is really up to the both of you."

"How so?" They both asked at once.

Walter smiled at his sister and Kelly thought inadvertently of a viper. "In the original will, you may remember, you get the foundry and I get $50,000 bucks. Dad has since changed his will in my favor since we assumed you were dead. At the moment, I get the foundry and you get nothing."

"I don't care what I get," Kelly returned savagely. "I just want to cast. I don't care if all I am is a hired hand."

Walter snorted his disbelief. "Then why not cast anywhere? Why come back home?"

"Why shouldn't I come back to...where I belong?" Kelly's face flushed with anger. Dave set a cup of coffee down in front of her. "Easy, Nancy," he soothed. "Take it easy. Have a bearclaw or a danish."

Kelly waved Dave's offer of food away. "Walter," she declared, leaning forward, her voice only a shade calmer, "I'm not here to take the foundry away from you."

Before Walter could make a rejoinder, they were both startled by a snort of laughter from Jim.

"What now?" Walter growled, turning to look at his father.

"That's my girl!" Jim crowed. "She's willing to work her way up from the bottom to earn the damn foundry! Are you up to the challenge, Walter?"

"Dad," Walter leaned menacingly toward the old man in the wheelchair, "are you planning to change the will?"

"Damn right, I'm gonna change the will, Walter. I have to account for a 'dead' person who's no longer dead!"

"Dad, how are you going to change the will?"

"I don't know yet, son. I have to give it some thought. My attorney's coming out this afternoon and I'm going to get her advice. That's what attorneys are for, after all."

"Dad," Kelly begged, "don't do anything rash."

"Don't worry, honey. I'm not going to do anything rash. Walter here will get his due."

Dave and Kelly shared a veiled look. Their worry was that neither of them knew exactly what Walter was 'due'.

Kelly spent the remainder of the morning in the office going through accounts, expressing recognition at those Dave had had her memorize and updating herself on the activity on those accounts that had evolved since Nancy would have seen them last.

Under Dave's tutelage and Jim's assessing eye, she focused on learning the customers who would have been new to Nancy and those, new and old, who had pieces in various stages of the casting process at the foundry.

She spent the afternoon in the foundry, trailing Rose and her latest customer, a rancher-artist named Penny Sidwell. Sidwell was a skinny, withered-up older woman with a bright eye, ready smile, and a firm handshake. She had hired the foundry to cast an intricate piece of a cowgirl throwing a saddle over her horse's back. Sidwell had modeled the original figure in clay and Rose was walking her through all of the steps the foundry would take to get her clay model to the point of a finished bronze.

Walter drifted in about ten minutes before Rose finished with Sidwell and pretended to talk to Jeff, who went on working, never raising his head. Once Sidwell headed out the door, Walter lost no time in coming over to talk to Rose. Rose's face, Kelly noticed, hardened as he approached, looking more like she wanted to punch him than that she welcomed his attentions.

"So, babe," he said, his voice familiar and confident, "do you want to go to dinner tonight?"

"No, Walter." Rose looked exasperated. "I'd rather not."

"Why not? We can even invite my sister along." Walter nodded at Kelly, his eyes alight with amusement which, once again, baffled Kelly. *What was Walter finding so funny about Nancy's return?*

Rose glanced at Kelly, her eyes dark and desperate, making Kelly think of a tiring swimmer sinking in a cold sea.

"Uh," Kelly hedged, aware of the tension and not wanting to make a misstep, "whatever you two want to do."

Rose dropped her head and her dark hair fell forward to cover her face. "Okay. Let's go to the Blue Corn. Are you going to pick us up?"

"Sure," Walter replied, grinning at his victory.

"I'll need to shower and change," Rose said.

Walter shrugged, glancing around the foundry. "Goes with the territory. I'll come by for you gals at 6:00."

By the time Walter pulled up to their door in his cherry red Mustang, Rose and Kelly were seated in the kitchen, too nervous to engage even in small talk. When they had first returned to the house, Kelly had laid on her bed listening to the muffled beat of the water running in the bathroom as Rose showered, trying to let the tensions and worries of the day melt away. She needed to be prepared for the next onslaught of questions: Walter's questions.

It was inevitable that he would test her in the absence of Dave and Jim and she wanted to get it over with. She felt that dreading Walter's asking her something she didn't know about from their childhood was more exhausting than fending off whatever he might actually throw at her.

In her opinion, facing his questions sooner was better than facing them later because the longer she lasted as Nancy, the less suspicious everyone would become, including Walter. She needed to secure Walter's belief in her identity now, early in the game.

There was the honk of Walter's horn and the women went out, Rose pulling shut and locking the door behind them. Kelly didn't yet have a key to the house.

Kelly climbed into the back seat of the Mustang, and after the seat back fell into place, Rose slid into the front. There was no sliding over to sit beside Walter on Rose's part although she offered him the most saccharine smile Kelly had ever seen.

"Cool," Walter said, like an ingenue in *Grease* and they were sailing out of the foundry entrance. "Hey, Sis," he called, "do you remember these wheels?"

"You didn't have this car, Walter," Kelly said coolly from the back seat. Walter laughed, but the sound was anxiously high-pitched. "Oh, yeah? So what car did I have?"

"Your disgusting apple green '68 Buick Skylark that you souped up and put lifters on. Whatever happened to that piece of junk anyway?" Kelly leaned companionably forward and noticed the dead white of Walter's knuckles against the red shine of the steering wheel.

Jeez, she thought to herself, *he was more nervous about this test than she was.*

"What a memory, sis!" He crowed enthusiastically, but Kelly could hear a trace of shakiness in his voice.

"Walter," Rose snarled, "why don't you just leave Nancy the hell alone? She's obviously your sister! I mean who else could she be?"

Walter laughed. "Hey," he said, his voice sounding normal again, "I just had to be sure. That's all. Okay? I won't ask any more leading questions."

"Promise?" Rose demanded. "Because I want to enjoy the evening. Not listen to the two of you play mind games."

"I promise."

At the Blue Corn, they were seated at a pleasant table near the fireplace. The restaurant's ambience was Southwestern bar-and-grille with pale pink stucco walls and grey slate floors. The wait staff was casually attired and laid back in their manner, but not so laid back as to irritate patrons.

After they had placed their orders, Kelly said, to break the ice, "So, Walter, why don't you fill me in on the last seven years."

Walter's face contorted. "Oh, very funny! What do you want? Just a quick summary?" His eyes glinted. "I have a better idea: why don't you fill *me* in on the last seven years? I'd be really interested to hear what happened to you."

"Actually, it's pretty boring. I just bummed around a lot, held a lot of different stupid jobs, and tried not to remember I had a home."

"But one day you did remember you had a home."

"Yeah. I guess I grew up enough to admit it. Sounds stupid, doesn't it?"

"Sounds like a modern prodigal son story to me, with a gender twist," Walter sneered. "Lost daughter remembers Daddy is rich and, if she plays her cards right, can come home to his loving arms. How did you feel when you saw he couldn't use those loving arms anymore?"

"Walter!" Rose shrieked. "That is cruel. You are so vicious!"

"It's all right, Rose." Kelly had a sudden insight into Walter's relationship with his sister and she decided to take a chance. "Walter was always like this. We fought like cats and dogs, didn't we, sib?"

"You're damn right we did. And I'm so glad you're back so we can take it up again." His sharply-pointed eye teeth showed as he grinned and Kelly was felt a rush of cold dislike raise goose bumps along her upper arms. It was becoming clear Walter was the kind of unsavory male personality who wasn't going to win any gentleman contests. But how deep was his real antagonism?

Their gigantic green chile cheeseburgers arrived and they all dug in. Kelly would have expected that, if Walter and Rose were dating, that they would at least exchange a few coy looks, if not remarks. Yet all she observed as they made their way through their meal were keyed-up looks on Walter's part directed toward her and a sort of all-pervading glower from Rose, who avoided as much as possible looking at either of them.

"Well, this was fun," Kelly forced herself to say after she had swallowed down the last of her burger. "We should definitely do it again." There was nothing she wanted more than to get out of the restaurant and out of their company.

To her astonishment, Walter demanded separate checks of the waiter, which left Rose and Kelly to pay for their own food. Kelly wasn't surprised he hadn't paid for her but he was the one who had insisted on going out and Rose was, after all, his girlfriend. He should have paid for her meal. Kelly was steamed enough to start a fight with him on Rose's behalf but Rose, if anything, seemed relieved by the turn of events.

On the way out to the car, Kelly muttered closely into the other woman's ear: "Why in hell do you go out with such a major jerk?"

Rose shivered and pulled her jacket more closely around her shoulders, but didn't reply. Walter was unlocking the passenger door of the Mustang and Rose gave him a wide conciliatory smile before pulling the seat forward for Kelly to slide into the back.

Kelly was still raging internally about Walter's behavior but there was nothing she could say or do. She had to remind herself that people had very bizarre relationships and if a relationship with an asshole like Walter was what Rose wanted, she would support her in it.

You never knew what people wanted in a partner. Forcing herself to forget about it, she shrugged and settled back against the seat for the short return ride to the foundry.

She was so tired after the big meal that she was almost dozing when Walter pulled up in front of the modular. Much to her surprise, Rose practically leaped from the vehicle, without a word to Walter, and dashed up the front steps.

Kelly, baffled again, pushed the seat forward and stepped out of the car, her mouth opening in a wide yawn. Had she actually fallen asleep and missed something Rose said? Something telling like 'I'm breaking up with you, Walter?'

And why was there no shared goodnight kiss? Or plans for

other, more romantic, gymnastics? She shrugged again, desperately needing sleep and no longer really caring about Walter's and Rose's relationship.

"Well, goodnight, Walter," she said through the open passenger window as she closed the door.

"Goodnight to you, sis," he called, giving her once again that feral grin. "Sleep tight and don't let them bed bugs bite."

She waved him away and went up the steps of her new home and inside, locking the door behind her. Rose was nowhere to be seen but her bedroom door was shut.

Kelly went immediately to bed. It was only in that last moment of consciousness before she fell into a deep slumber that she realized Walter had not called her 'Nancy'.

The next few weeks swam by Kelly's overwrought conscious-

EIGHT

ness in much the same way that a person learning a new and complex job retains some things and forgets others, performs well in some areas and absolutely flounders in others. Her daily hope was that she didn't flounder where it mattered.

The small foundry 'family' seemed largely to have gotten over the shock of her presence and were beginning to fall into a routine that either included or avoided her as they saw fit. Dave continued to train her daily in the business accounts, Jim to oversee her progress with all factors of the business including the technical steps involved in casting, Rose to stay as far away from her as possible, and Walter to needle or harass her at every opportunity.

She and Rose had fallen into a pattern of eating breakfast and lunch at different times so that they were unlikely to run into each other in any private face-to-face settings. Kelly was usually expected to show up for dinner at Jim's and Alice's but

Rose, as an employee, was not. Walter came for dinner two or three times a week when he felt like it and without providing advance notice. Alice always accommodated him without comment.

Kelly liked those evenings least. She didn't know if it was because Walter set her more on edge or he set all of them more on edge. Dave came frequently to dinner for the first several weeks, but seeing Kelly's progress with the family and quickly running out of excuses for hanging around, began to taper off his presence. In particular, he avoided meals that included Walter.

In the third week of her employment, Rose turned over two new design customers to Kelly with the tart comment, "Jim said these were yours to handle."

Neither of the accounts were large or artistically significant. Neither were for clients who were likely to be repeat business. Neither were for long-term customers who would have known or cared about the original Nancy or who had a long-term commitment to the foundry.

It became immediately clear to Kelly that Jim Summerhill wanted a trial run out of her before he took the risk of introducing his new-found daughter to the significant members of the local art community. She guessed he needed to know with certainty that she was good before the word spread that she had returned and the business that had started to fall off under Walter's mismanagement started to rebuild as a result of the confidence generated by the community's memory of the real Nancy's potential.

Deep in her gut, Kelly knew her future with the foundry rode on these two apparently insignificant accounts. One was for the repair of the handle of an antique sword and the other was for a one-of-a-kind family memorabilia trophy of a bullmoose head.

Kelly went about her new commitments with a mixture of trepidation and concentration. She would have to set up an appointment with the owner of the sword, study the sword's venue and, based on its period and style, redesign and cast the lost piece, then determine how it should be treated to seamlessly match the original sword's patina.

For the trophy, she would have to design the bullmoose head herself (the request had been made by the family, not an artist), estimate materials and labor costs, check that she had enough supplies, establish completion time frames, create the clay models, and assist Atavema with the molds.

If everything wasn't done perfectly, blowholes could mar the final bronze result and she would have to start over. After pouring, if all went well, she would have to walk the piece through the customer's specifications for finishing, communicating closely at every stage with Jeff about the finishing work he did.

Last but not least, she needed to determine how much to charge each of her customers and, most important of all, get them to pay the bill.

Late one afternoon after Atavema and Jeff had left for the day, Kelly sat in the Clay Enlargement and Reduction section of the foundry happily adding more clay to the bullmoose head she had designed based loosely on a photo torn from a magazine that the family had approved of the intended object.

When she was doing this kind of focused work, time passed without her knowledge of it. She had been at it for a long time when she was startled out of her absorption by the sound of raised voices at the rear of the foundry.

"I don't give a shit anymore!" Rose was shouting. "Just leave me alone!"

"He'll fire your ass!"

Kelly recognized the responding voice as Walter's.

"He's going to fire me anyway! Once Nancy is up and running, I won't have a job! So, keep your damp hands and slimy mouth away from me, you sick pervert!"

Kelly had stopped working and was looking in the direction of the voices but she couldn't see the two combatants, who were out of her view behind the concrete wall that contained the ceramic baths and the pouring section.

After the last remark, she saw Rose come tearing out from behind the wall. She was brushing slag and grit from her pants and her face was the color of raspberries. Walter followed her, a scowl marring his forehead.

"You'll regret this, Rose!" He called after her.

"What I regret," she screamed, without looking back over her shoulder, "is the first moment I ever saw you and this evil place!"

Kelly watched Rose's angry progress down the wide central aisle of the foundry. Her head was down, her fists swung clenched beside her hips, her black curls bounced with outrage, and Kelly could just catch the scattered sheen of light on her cheeks that showed she was crying. Rose reached the front door and exited the building, slamming the heavy metal door behind her.

Kelly hesitated. Should she go after Rose and offer some comfort? Should she stay out of it and get back to her work? Or should she tell off Walter for his rude ways?

Walter, she saw, had stopped dead in his tracks, noticing for the first time that Kelly was still in the foundry. A moment later, it was clear from his expression that he had figured out she had overheard the altercation. He stood looking at her, a sneer on his face, almost as if he were daring her to say something. Slowly, he walked toward her.

When he was no more than five feet away, his face contorted into an angry mask, he spat out two words at her: "Fucking queer." Then he simply walked on, as if nothing had happened.

Kelly was stunned into speechlessness. By the time she'd gathered her wits to respond, Walter was gone. She rushed to the door of the foundry, but there was no one in sight in the parking lot or around the corner of the building. She went back into the foundry, and closed the door. She leaned against it, trembling.

When she had first come out to her parents, they had said nothing directly condemning. There had been no shouting or recriminations or pleading on their part or on hers. They had simply asked her to leave their home and not return. There had been no discussion and no negotiations. They had turned her a cold shoulder and that had been the end of it.

She had never experienced vituperative 'in your face' hatred for being gay. It made her feel cold and dirty and numb. Eventually, she straightened up, obsessively wiping away Walter's nonexistent spittle from her shirt and walked back to sit in front of the bullmoose head model.

For a moment, the clay figure disappeared behind the rage that suddenly welled up in her body and blinded her eyes. She almost reached out to grab it and throw it to the floor. Instead, she lunged for some unmolded clay and started battering it with her hands.

After a few moments of violent pounding, she calmed down and went back to adding clay to the bullmoose head. In less than ten strokes though, the figure started to distort and Kelly knew she wasn't going to be able to do any more work on it for the remainder of the evening. She was too distraught. Giving up, she turned off the lights, locked the door, and left the building.

At home, Rose's bedroom door, as usual, was closed. Tiredly, Kelly got into a hot shower and let the water pound on the back of her neck until she felt some of the deadness drain away. After the shower, she changed into clean jeans and a sweater. The October nights were getting cooler.

She went out into the kitchen and stared into the refrigerator. Her food stores were adequate but she didn't see anything she thought she could eat. Her stomach was as tight as a drum.

She drifted back down the hall toward her bedroom. At Rose's closed door, she hesitated and stopped to listen to see if any sounds emanated from the other woman's room. She thought she heard a low pained moaning.

After a few long moments, during which she struggled with her conscience, she opened the door and looked in. Rose was laying on the bed, her face buried in a pillow but her sobs were still vocal enough to be heard.

Kelly entered the room and sat down on the edge of the bed. "He's just not worth it," she whispered, reaching out to stroke Rose's hair. Rose's body went completely still and then she started sobbing again.

"Forget about him," Kelly whispered. "He's an asshole."

"I know he's an asshole," Rose sobbed. "But there's nothing I can do about it."

"Sure there is. Just tell him to stay away from you. Better yet, start dating some other guy. That'll get the message across."

"Oh, god," Rose moaned. "You just don't get it, do you, Nancy?"

"Get what? Oh, my god. Are you in love with that turd Walter?"

Rose's whole body shook. She rolled over onto her back and twisted her body away from Kelly.

"In love with him? Are you out of your mind!"

"Okay. So, you're not in love with him. So, what's the big problem?"

"Oh, lord!" Rose clutched a pillow to her stomach and staggered off the bed, looking like she might throw up. "I'm gay, you idiot! Isn't that obvious to you?"

Kelly felt as though she'd been punched in the solar plexus. Her breath just wouldn't come into her lungs. When it did, she gasped and sputtered.

"What?"

Rose continued to clutch the pillow to her body, as if expecting to fend off blows, and gaped at Kelly. "You're gay, aren't you?"

"Yeah, but...then...what's all this with Walter?"

"Your dad is a complete homophobe! Because of you, I might add! Didn't you know that?"

"Uh," Kelly frowned, remembering what Dave had told her, "I still don't get what this has to do with Walter."

"Walter's my cover. Are you dense or something?"

"Do you mean to tell me...wait. Does Walter know you're gay?"

"Of course Walter knows I'm gay!"

Kelly felt her stomach turn over. The man hated queers, she knew that for a fact. There had been nothing conciliatory or nicey-nice about the way he had spat the words 'fucking queer' at her.

"Are you completely sane? Are you telling me Walter knows you're gay and he pursues you anyway? You let him do it?"

"He's supposed to be pretending to be dating me. It's not as if I let him get into my pants or anything. It's so your dad won't find out I'm queer and fire me."

"Shit. I don't think Walter's pretending."

"I'm beginning to wonder that myself. Still, up until now, he hasn't tried to get too physical with—"

Kelly felt a deep stirring of disgust in her body. She couldn't keep from interrupting Rose. "Are you telling me that screaming match I witnessed in the foundry is part of some *game*?" Now she wondered if Walter's 'fucking queer' remark had even been directed at her. Maybe it had been directed at Rose instead.

"No. That was real. Walter's starting to become a pain in the ass about our dating arrangement. He was more willing to be hands off before you came. Now he's starting to get kind of...obsessed. I don't know why but he's beginning to creep me out."

"This entire scenario is creeping me out."

"Well, you can just get off your high horse, Ms. Summerhill! Some of us don't have dads who own foundries! Some of us have to keep our orientations to ourselves so we can keep our jobs! But since you're daddy's little girl, you don't have to worry about it!"

Kelly wasn't sure for a minute which emotions predominated in her body. There were so many: anger at the truths, however misguided, in Rose's statement; burgeoning resentment about having to hide not just her orientation but her real self from everyone; secret delight in discovering that Rose was gay; perturbation that she couldn't pursue a relationship with her since she had promised Dave she would maintain a facade of 'reform'; loathing at Walter for humiliating Rose; rage at Jim for being so narrow-minded...so many thoughts whirled through her brain, she began to feel dizzy. So dizzy, she lost her balance and slid off the bed.

The next thing she knew, Rose was kneeling beside her and shaking her hard by the shoulder. "Nancy!"

Her head spun woozily. "What happened?"

"I don't know. I think you passed out for a second. You scared the hell out of me."

Kelly looked up into Rose's beautiful, worried, hazel eyes. "Have dinner with me."

They found themselves at a quiet Chinese restaurant on the Cerrillos Road strip that strove to create a mystical ambience with soft, toneless Chinese music, weepy greenery, bowing young wait staff, and colorful imitations of dreamy Chinese scroll paintings.

They both ordered big bowls of steaming hot won ton soup. Kelly figured it was the only thing she would be able to get into her stomach. The soup was as soothing and easy to eat as she had hoped it would be and when she had finished it, she realized she was ravenously hungry. Rose was in the same mood and, laughing, they ordered more food: chow mein, fried rice, and hefty steamed pork dumplings.

"I'm sorry," Kelly said, when they had dug in to the second half of their order. "I wasn't trying to be dense about you. I was trying to not have anything to do with you so that—"

Rose smiled encouragingly. "So that?"

Kelly couldn't exactly reveal that she had made a deal with Dave. "I guess so that I didn't irritate my father like I did the first time around."

"Do you find me attractive?" Rose asked.

Kelly broke out into a light sweat. *Was this woman crazy? Attractive didn't cover it.* She thought she had never seen Rose so relaxed, and relaxed only made her ten times sexier.

Her perfectly-shaped body was stretched languidly against the back of the cushioned red booth and she sipped tea from a porcelain cup held delicately between her lon,g graceful fingers.

"Rose, you're more than attractive. But aren't we rushing things here a bit? What about your job, for instance?"

"I really do believe your dad will fire me any day now, Nancy." Rose straightened up and went back to serious eating.

"Why?"

"Why will he need me?" Rose wiped her mouth on a napkin. "Once you've proven to him that you can run the place—and I'm sure you can already do it—he'll let me go. Those two commissions are the handwriting on the wall for me."

"You don't think I should intentionally fuck those up, do you?"

"What?" Rose looked up from her food, startled. "Of course not! Nancy, get smart! The foundry is yours! Your dad is wetting his pants with sheer excitement on a daily basis over your return. If he could move, he'd be dancing on the frigging rooftops."

"Damn it, Rose! I just don't see how that means it's curtains for you! If it's my damn foundry, like you say, I'll keep you on!"

"Nancy, let's go one day at a time here and be rational about it. You've been poring over the accounts for weeks now. I have too, in the past, and I can tell you there are only a few viable economic options for the foundry."

She started to count off on her fingers. "One. Get rid of me or, two, get rid of Walter or, three, drum up about $40,000 more business per year. There's no way to do the second one and the only way to do the last one is to start casting bigger pieces. The industry and the taste of the public is going in the way of more monumental castings. That leaves the first option as the simplest, quickest and most sensible one, considering you've arrived and are perfectly able to fill my shoes as the foundry manager. Summerhill Foundry is just never going to be big enough to require two foundry managers."

"Damn it, Rose. I agree with your summary but I don't buy

your solution. There has to be more than one way to skin this cat."

"Like what?"

"Like option two or three. Besides, what would you do if you left the foundry?"

"Oh, I don't know. Just getting away from Walter would be a blessing all by itself."

"Do you want to go?"

"No. I'm just trying to adjust myself to the reality of it."

"What if we did go after the monumental market? What would we have to do differently?"

"Well, in terms of equipment, not a lot at first but we'd have to cast works in more sections than a big foundry because our furnace and our ladle aren't big enough to pour huge sections with one pour. There'd be a greater initial cost for basic supplies like clay and wax and, of course, bronze. In terms of labor, we'd all be running around like madmen trying to get it done within time frames. That Stacy Allcraft piece I did was one hell of a challenge."

"Did you enjoy it?"

"Loved it."

"Would you do it again?"

"You bet."

"Would you do something for the first time?" Kelly's voice had turned low and coy.

Rose looked at her, her eyebrows rising slightly. "It depends on what it is and, if it's what I'm thinking it is, it wouldn't be the first time."

"It would be the first time with me."

Rose's mouth quirked as she laid down her fork. "Do you think they would put the rest of our dinner in a doggy bag?"

Rose didn't turn on the kitchen light when they got back to

NINE

the house. Grasping Nancy's wrist, she led her down the darkened hallway they both knew well and into her bedroom. Even there, she only turned on the closet light which shed a soft unintrusive glow around the room.

She kicked off her shoes and motioned for Nancy to do the same. Then she sat on the bed and drew Nancy toward her until the other woman's legs were between her outstretched thighs. She ran her hands down Nancy's back and over her hips. Nancy shivered in excitement.

Rose unsnapped Nancy's jeans and eased the zipper down. Other than their breathing, it was the only sound in the room. Next came the slither of Nancy's jeans as Rose slipped them off her hips and pushed them down her legs. Rose laid back on the bed, pulling Nancy with her, stroking the silky softness of her thighs.

Her mouth met Nancy's in a soft exploratory kiss, that ripe

full sensation of another woman's lips on her own exciting her like no other aphrodisiac. She rolled Nancy over on her back and started to kiss her like someone who hadn't tasted that kind of lusciousness in a very long while. And it had been a very long while. Two years, at least. Maybe three.

Kelly returned Rose's urgency, kiss for kiss, tongue for tongue. Eventually, they were both panting, the excitement generated by their mouths and hands transferring to other, even more tender, aspects of their anatomy. Kelly rolled Rose onto her back and had begun a slow kiss-fraught slide down Rose's neck.

Soon, she was nestling her lips in that delicate enticing cavern between Rose's breasts, tasting salt and sweat and inhaling the warm moist scent of Rose's skin. With sure fingers, she unbuttoned Rose's shirt and unsnapped her bra, thrusting both aside. The sight of Rose's full naked breasts, with their soft pink aureoles and erect nipples, sent messages to every part of Kelly's body: hands, fingers, tongue, clitoris, all of which were tingling and ravenous for sensation.

Her mouth devoured each nipple in turn, tonguing and sucking and nibbling until Rose's moans formed a cascade of ooh's and aah's tumbling over an erotic Niagra of arousal. She moved down Rose's body, moistening her belly with her tongue, until she reached the top of her jeans.

There, without undoing the snap or zipper, she boldly slipped her hand inside Rose's panties, past the soft full curls, into the slippery wetness between her thighs.

Rose arched and cried out, "Oh, my god."

Kelly's hand stilled in preparation for an even bigger plunge into Rose's soft territory. "Are you ready for me, baby?"

"Oh, god, Nancy. Don't stop there!"

The calling out of a name not her own shocked Kelly into

temporary paralysis. The hiatus lasted so long Rose raised her head from the bed. "Is everything okay?"

"Uh, yeah," Kelly came back to life. "I just need to—" she stalled, slipping her hand out of Rose's pants, "—undo your jeans here. Won't take a second." She slid off the bed and unzipped Rose's jeans, still struggling to regain her concentration. *What difference did it make whose name Rose called? She, Kelly, was the one taking her. It was the same her no matter what Rose called her.*

She pulled Rose's jeans from her legs, exposing the womanly shape of her long thighs and calves. The sight helped Kelly to focus. *God, but Rose was gorgeous.* She was gorgeous and she was hot. Hot, desperate and begging for Kelly to bring her to the point of ecstasy.

Kelly swallowed hard in her excitement and pulled Rose's soaked panties from her, releasing the musky sweet smell of a woman whose body was ready, very ready, to respond to Kelly's every touch, every ministration. Kelly knelt between Rose's legs and slipped her tongue into the hot creamy center of Rose's being, beginning a slow torturous stroking of all of Rose's most delicate places.

Rose was panting, panting hard and moaning.

"Please, Nancy, please." Kelly continued the actions of her tongue and then slowly brought her fingers up to caress Rose's opening. Without resistance, but with a gasp from Rose, she slipped three fingers inside, bringing Rose to an even higher plane of arousal.

Kelly drove her fingers in and out, attentive to the tight heat of Rose's body and wetness of her hand, and the feeling it added to her own sensation of heat and wetness. Her own panties, she knew, were soaked. With a rending cry, Rose climaxed, her body arching on the bed, the pulsing in her body seeming to engulf Kelly's mouth and hand.

Kelly got up off the floor and joined Rose on the bed, cradling her in her arms. "You are one hot mama," Kelly whispered in her ear.

"And you are one red hot lover, girlfriend." Rose moved her head to nestle between Kelly's still-clad breasts. They weren't clad for long as Rose went to work unbuttoning Kelly's shirt. Kelly didn't wear a bra, her breasts being mostly compact, and Rose brought her nipples to instant erection just by grazing them with her fingers. Kelly moaned and lay flat, letting her lover decide what she wanted to do with her.

Rose drew her curled hair across Kelly's breasts and Kelly went breathless. Rose's hair had held her entranced for weeks: its bounce, the softness of its curls, the rich dark color making her think of the night sky and polished ebony. *If only...*

As if she'd read her mind, Rose was there between her legs, teasing the skin of Kelly's thighs with her hair. Before Kelly noticed, she had yanked Kelly's panties from her and was drawing the soft darkness of her hair against Kelly's naked pubis.

Kelly gasped. Rose's hair would smell of her arousal and it would be difficult to look at her and not think of it, not be aroused all over again by it. Kelly's throat was dry with her excitement.

She felt Rose's fingers thrusting into her and her thumb reaching for her clitoris. In less than two strokes of Rose's hand, Kelly came in an explosion of sensation, her body rocketing skyward and then falling unresisting into the soft dewy down of the bed.

When Kelly awakened, she came to the slow groggy realization that she was in Rose's bed. Rose was not beside her but, despite that, recollection of the evening's events came back to her mind in a quick intoxicating rush. She had been so uninhibited, so turned on. It wasn't her usual style. In fact, she hadn't been with a woman for a good three years, not even for a safe-sex quickie in a women's bar's bathroom.

Her last lover had not been particularly impressed with either Kelly's poverty or her open-road style of living and had tolerated traveling with her for less than two weeks. The conditions, Kelly reflected, had been hard. Not the kind of state that lead to erotic encounters, let alone life partners.

But everything was different now. Kelly sat up in the bed and stretched languidly. She felt renewed, as though all the tension she had been holding for months had been released by last night's lovemaking. She hadn't realized until this moment how much strain it was to pretend to be someone else. Not that she could stop pretending but...her eyes scanned the digital clock perched on the headboard: 9:21.

Shit! She had a design customer at 9:30. Kelly leaped from the bed and dashed nude into the hall and directly into the shower. With no time to dry her hair, she pulled on a pair of clean jeans and a flannel cowboy shirt. She was meeting Edmund White, the son of the man for whom the bullmoose head was to be a surprise at his 30th wedding anniversary.

Edmund was already inside the foundry and viewing with suspicion her version of the bullmoose head when she arrived. Jeff was torching a finished bronze to heat it in preparation for applying a coating of corrosives. Atavema was brushing liquefied silicone over the prepared clay hull of a full-masted sailing galleon—which would have to be cast in multiple pieces—and Rose, much to Kelly's disappointment, was nowhere in sight.

Kelly glanced at her watch. It was 9:33. Poor form, but not late enough to get her reprimanded, except by herself. If she was going to be head of the foundry someday, she would need to be more conscientious. Women, no matter how provocative, were going to have to come second.

"Well, Edmund," she asked, a little out of breath, "what do you think?"

"I think it's kind of lopsided. And now that I look at it, this just isn't going to be big enough. It needs to be heavier, more massive. More damn heroic."

"We can, of course," Kelly called upon her most diplomatic voice, "enlarge it. But it will add to the cost."

"How much?" Edmund snapped.

"How much bigger do you want it?"

"Oh, about 3 to 4 inches on all sides."

"Okay. Just eyeing it, I'd guess that's approximately a 25% increase in mass so we'll have to figure a corresponding 25% in cost. Remember, it's more everything: more clay, more silicone, more wax, more bronze, more patina."

"Damn. I don't want to go over budget on this thing, Nancy. But it's got to be bigger."

"Let me pull your contract and we'll amend it."

Edmund tapped one well-clad shoe on the concrete floor of the foundry, hesitating.

"Yes or no?" Kelly asked.

"Yes. All right."

"Good, then. Let's go up to the office." She escorted the barrel-chested man to the conference room which was in the main house near Jim's office. She pulled the White contract from the files, made the necessary alterations and had Edmund initial all of the changes. She attached an affidavit to it stating the date of the contract changes and had Alice come in and notarize her and Edmund's signatures.

They shook hands over the deal, Edmund finally with a smile on his round boisterous face, as he loudly proclaimed to her that he was happy with the changes and that he felt strongly that he had made the right decision in choosing Summerhill Foundry for the work.

After the man left, Jim Summerhill powered his way into the office. "Let me see the contract amendments," he demanded.

"Sure, Dad." She picked up the contract and took it over to him, snapping it onto a clipboard attachment on his wheelchair that put written material directly in front of his eyes. He scanned the contract, his chin high and critical, and then his body seemed to settle back into his chair.

"Nancy, this was a minor account. I didn't expect anything of it. And yet, you've already increased it by 25%. That is excellent!"

Kelly was startled. "It was entirely accidental, Dad. He wanted a larger bust than he originally ordered. Once he saw it, he knew it wasn't right. You know that happens sometimes."

"I don't care, at this stage, whether it was skill or luck, child. You are good for this foundry." With that, he reversed motor power with his chin and backed out of the office. Kelly stared after him, stupefied.

Still, as she went out, she hoped that what he had said would prove to be true.

That evening, Rose went into town at the end of the workday and bought T-bone steaks and fresh potatoes to fry up. She also splurged on a bottle of wine. She wanted, for the first time, to share dinner with Nancy in their own house.

Kelly, unaware of her lover's plans, stayed late in the foundry enlarging the bullmoose head. Rose came to get her as the sun started to sink toward the west, coloring the sky with an outrageous array of impossible shades.

"Hey," Kelly greeted her when she came in. "I got a late start on the day so I thought I owed it to the company."

"No, you didn't. You love being out here."

"I do love it." Kelly swiveled on the stool on which she sat. "But it's not all I love."

"Not too loudly," Rose hissed, her hands on her hips. "Are you going to come into dinner?"

"Are you inviting me?"

"Yes, I am."

Kelly needed no further urging. She jumped up and in a moment, they were both out the door. Kelly wanted to take Rose's hand as they crossed the parking lot but she knew it would be a mistake.

Much to the surprise of both of them, Walter's Mustang roared around the side of the foundry, fishtailed in front of them and left the lot, spewing gravel in all directions.

"That's weird," Rose commented, shielding her face from the flying rocks, "I thought he was long gone home. It's almost like he didn't see us."

"I thought he was gone, too. He gets to be more of a jerk every day. I wonder what he was doing lurking around back there. Say, you didn't say anything to him about us today, did you?"

Rose grimaced. "Are you crazy? Of course not."

"Have you told him you've broken up with him, yet?"

"No. Not unless our big fight in the foundry counted."

"Are you planning to tell him or are you going to continue to play him along?" They had reached the house and Kelly was holding the door open for Rose.

"I don't know, Nancy. Which do you think is safer?"

Kelly dropped her head to one side, thinking. "I don't know. Maybe it depends on how you define 'safe'."

"See, I don't know either and I've been thinking about it off and on all day."

They were in the kitchen and Kelly was awed. "Wow, this table is gorgeous! I didn't even know you had candles, Rose." There was a tall white tapered pair set in individual brass flower-shaped holders. The tablecloth was white linen. Between the candles sat an arrangement of red and white carnations and a statuesque bottle of red wine.

"The wine," Rose raised her eyebrows in an attempt at playing coy, "needs to be opened. The corkscrew is on the counter."

"I think I can manage it," Kelly said, her heart thumping with happiness. When it was opened, she poured a test measure for Rose, who drank it, looking deeply into Kelly's eyes. Kelly gently pulled the wineglass from Rose's fingers and settled it on the counter. Then she brought Rose into her arms for a kiss that lasted an eternity.

In their joy, both of them had quite entirely forgotten about Walter.

The acrid smell of the droplets of bronze slag that fell to the

TEN

concrete floor made Kelly's nostrils twitch. The heavy lined helmet blanketing her head and the clear plexiglass of her face mask protected her from flying sparks but not from inhaled smoke.

Despite the tangy atmosphere of heat and metal-tinged smoke, the steel roll-up door was firmly closed. Even something as gentle as an autumn breeze could overcool the molten bronze in the crucible and it would have to be reheated to enable it to be poured. So, despite the discomfort to the pouring crew, the door remained closed during actual pours.

The skin beneath the cushioned headband of Kelly's mask itched but she couldn't stop to rub it with her fingers—even if they hadn't been encased in flame-retardant gloves—because both of her aching arms were occupied swinging the pallet bearing a clay mold into place in the sand pit. Sweat was soaking the muscle shirt and jeans she wore beneath her flame-retardant suit, making her skin sticky and damp.

The heat, the itchy tingle of sweat trickling between her thighs, and the heavy slickness of her skin reminded her of the evenings she'd been spending with Rose. Rose's hair, dark against the bedspread, Rose's full naked breasts, Rose's sculpted belly and hips...

"Hey!"

Startled, Kelly brought her focus back to the job at hand. She had nearly overshot the sand pit. Walter had punched the stop button on the automated pulley. "What the hell do you think you're doing?"

"Sorry," she shouted over the blasting noise of the furnace, "spaced out."

"You can't space out in here! It's a damn good thing we weren't swinging the crucible around. If you space out with that, the damage will be permanent."

Even behind his scarred face mask, Kelly could see Walter's heavy scowl. She looked at the crucible, which was shaped like a sand bucket children took to the beach, except that it was molded from iron and many thousands of times heavier. Its interior had been flamed to a hot orange glow with a torch so that the molten bronze wouldn't cool excessively when it came into contact with it.

Walter was right. If the bronze-bearing crucible spilled, the bronze would burn right through her clothes, fire-retardant suit or not. It was heavy too and the sheer weight of it, if it slammed into someone, could kill.

Kelly heard the whir of the machinery overhead and adrenaline shot through her body as her hands steadied the frame of iron rebar from which the metal pallet swung. Her muscles straining, she guided the pallet back to the sand pit. As she held it steady, Walter activated the pulley system to lower the pallet into place.

The next step would be to pour the molten bronze from the furnace into the crucible. Once that was done, the crucible would be attached to a wheel-operated frame and maneuvered around the sand pit with the automated pulley system, stopping to fill each clay riser of the mold with a bright orange river of bronze.

She walked away from the sand pit to pick up the electronic temperature gauge. The undemonstrative Jeff, to her surprise, patted her on the shoulder and then walked over to help Walter pour the bronze from the furnace into the crucible.

When it was poured, she would thrust the gauge into the molten bronze to check its temperature. If they had done everything correctly, it would read above 2000 degrees. The few minutes it would take to attach it to the frame after pouring it into the crucible would further drop its furnace heat. She would then re-test and when the bronze was exactly 2000 degrees, they would pour it into the molds.

The molds they were pouring today was in two parts: the first section had been the head of a ½ life size statue of a female bust and this second pour was the torso. The fired clay mold waiting in the sand pit was not recognizable as a bust or anything else. It looked most like a 3-D version of a Dr. Seuss drawing of some new-fangled musical instrument, all flared tubes and loops and hollows.

The two men had attached the filled crucible to its pulley-operated frame and Walter signaled Kelly to bring the temperature gauge over. The gauge was on a long hollow pole, angled at the end. Walter slipped a clean cover over its tip and Kelly thrust it into the bronze. Her red digital readout blinked 2018. Walter flicked off the bronze-encrusted gauge cover and the men swung the crucible into place over a riser of the clay mold.

Walter repeated the process and Kelly's readout blinked 2005. Walter nodded his head at Jeff and the tall laconic man began to pull on the wheel that would take the crucible from an upright position and slowly tilt it.

Kelly held her breath as Walter steadied the crucible directly over the fluted riser. A moment later, she saw the liquid bronze flow from the crucible into the riser, making her think of the hot orange tail of a comet. When the riser was full, the bronze spurted from its full top like a shower of hot stars.

It was already Kelly's fifth pour at Summerhill but the process still excited her. She couldn't wait for the day—which would be soon—when she was the one manning the crucible's wheel.

Walter grunted and nodded and Jeff turned the wheel back, bringing the crucible to an upright position. Then the two men swung the crucible over the next riser and repeated the process. A total of four risers completed this particular pour.

When they were done with all four, they swung the now-empty crucible back into position beside the furnace and Walter went immediately to tug on the chain that rolled up the metal door and which would allow in the cooler air from outside. Jeff turned off the furnace and the sudden silence was as much a shock to Kelly's ears as the breeze now filling the room was to her sweat-slicked body.

Walter ripped off his head mask and started unsnapping his flame retardant suit. He stood at the door, breathing in deep gulps of clean air. Kelly stripped out of her mask and suit and piled them in an aluminum bin labeled 'Gear'. Her muscle shirt was soaked through with sweat and she could feel metal grit between her breasts. She ruffled her hands through the damp strands of her clumping hair and a dirty smell of smoke floated around her head.

It was time to take a shower. The men neither looked at her or spoke to her as she left. In the modular, she headed directly for the bathroom, dumping her filthy clothes in the hamper which was piled high with both her and Rose's clothes. Clearly, it was laundromat night. Kelly wasn't even sure what she had left that she could wear because she hadn't had much to start with anyway.

She had spent her first bi-weekly check on two front tires for her truck. They had been so bald she had begun to worry about a blowout. When she got her second check, she hoped she might be able to buy a couple of used jeans at a thrift store, some new underwear to replace her tatters, and restock some of the food stores that Rose had been sharing with her, without pointing out the obvious—that it was her turn to buy.

Maybe she could even afford something for Rose...the shower water poured over Kelly's shoulders, cleansing the grit and sweat and smoke from her body. She turned to run her hair under the cascade of water and heard a distant thud like that of the front door slamming.

Maybe it was Rose, back from her run to the hardware store to pick up sanding discs and a backlog of other supplies for the foundry. Kelly smiled to herself and closed her eyes. Maybe Rose would come in and find her naked in the shower...they hadn't acted out that particular fantasy yet.

In her mind's eye, Kelly could see Rose's clothes and hair running with water and starting to cling to the gorgeous contours of her body. Would she help Rose out of her wet shirt and reach to peel her damp jeans from her thighs? Kelly could feel herself drowning in Rose's smooth wet mouth.

Kelly heard a second thud and awoke from her fantasy. She turned off the water and toweled herself dry. If it was Rose, she'd come and gone. Kelly heard a third thud. What in heck was going on?

With the towel cinched around her breasts, she stepped out of the bathroom and scanned the hallway. There was no one there. She walked out to the kitchen. Likewise, it was empty. She shrugged and headed back to her room.

At the door, she winced in shock. On top of her bedspread lay one of her kiln-fired pottery works, smashed to bits. The piece was one of her favorites: an innocently-smiling girl holding a disgruntled cat out in front of her body that, hanging as it was in the air, was almost as tall as the child. It was whimsical and unique, and would have brought her at least $250 at an art show.

Kelly moved toward the bed, tears smarting in her eyes. How had Kitty's Pride ended up on the bed? How had it gotten smashed? Had something fallen on it? She didn't see anything heavy amid the wreckage. She lifted part of the girl's head and arm and cradled it against her body, the tears flowing in earnest down her cheeks. How had this happened?

She lifted part of the cat's body and beneath it saw a flutter of white in one of the troughs of the aqua bedspread. It was a scrap of folded notebook paper that had been torn from a full sheet. She opened it. Scrawled inside in uneven red ink were the words *watch out.*

Kelly dropped the smashed bits of pottery and the piece of paper like they were on fire. She rose slowly from the bed staring in horror at the now-upturned scrap of white.

Kelly shuddered with a sudden sense of chill and nervously cinched her towel more tightly around her body. Who could have done this?

It was so infantile to smash something...and therefore all the more frightening. Who would go to such idiotic lengths to frighten her? And what in the hell was she supposed to watch out for?

Kelly's tears of sorrow turned to tears of frustration. Things had been going so well! No one knew who she was...no one, that is, but Dave. Everyone else had accepted her lock, stock and barrel as Nancy Summerhill.

Why would Dave try to frighten her? Kelly stripped off her towel and pulled on underwear, her last pair of clean jeans and a denim work shirt, feeling a sudden surge of angry energy. Who did Dave think he was anyway? Did he think this was a cute way to warn her to be more careful? Had she slipped up somewhere and he'd noticed?

After stuffing her jeans with her wallet and truck keys, Kelly was out the door. She might have to drive all the way downtown, but she wasn't going to let that keep her from giving Dave Paxton a piece of her mind.

When she got to Sena Plaza, she leaped the stairs to Dave's office two at a time. When she burst into his office, he was on the phone. Seeing the enraged look on her face, he asked the caller if he could call them back and hung up. Then he rose from behind his table and came toward her.

"What is the matter?"

"Why did you do that? What were you thinking? And by the way, you now owe me $250 bucks." Kelly could feel the allegorical steam pumping out of her ears.

"What? What are you talking about? What happened?"

"Why don't you explain, since you're the one who did it?"

"Did what?"

"Dave, I have been being careful. What kind of childish nonsense were you trying to pull?"

Dave frowned. "Kelly, why don't you start at the beginning? Go slowly."

"Jeez, what a smartass. I'm talking about Kitty's Pride!"

"Kitty Pride. Isn't that a brand of cat litter box sand?"

"Not Kitty Pride! Kitty's Pride! My piece! It's a girl holding a cat. You smashed it!"

"Excuse me?" Dave straightened. "You're accusing me of breaking one of your pieces? Why in the hell would I do something like that?"

"You think I'm screwing up somewhere! You were trying to make a point." She thrust the scrap of paper at him and Dave took it. His face paled when he read the print.

"Watch out," he mumbled, his eyes going to the floor. "Shit. That isn't good."

"Couldn't you have just told me?"

"Told you what?" Dave seemed to come back from wherever he'd been. "Oh, Kelly, for god's sake, you're doing a great job. And if I thought you were screwing up, I sure as hell wouldn't write you a damn fool note like this and break one of your pieces! That's the most idiotic thing I've ever heard!"

"Well, then...oh, god," Kelly fell back toward a chair and sat down. "Then someone else knows."

Dave frowned, the furrows in his brow deep and angry. "This is incredibly nasty. Where was the note?"

"Under Kitty's Pride."

"Where was Kitty's Pride?"

"On my bed."

"On your bed?" Dave's eyebrows rose into his hairline.

"Does that mean something to you?"

"No, but it might to the perpetrator. A bed is a very intimate spot. Angry lovers have been know to despoil their ex-lovers beds."

"Rose would never do something like that and beside we're hardly ex..."

"Shit! Are you already sleeping with Rose?"

Kelly's head had been down but now she raised it defiantly. "Dave, you stay the fuck out of my sex life!"

"I'm very happy to stay out of your sex life, Kelly. But clearly, somebody else isn't." He waggled the piece of paper at her.

"Oh, hell," Kelly got up and started to pace away from him, "there's absolutely no way for anyone to know. I mean how could they? We're only romantic after dark, after everyone else has left the foundry, or gone to bed."

Dave's lips compressed into a thin line and he stared hard at Kelly's retreating back. "I thought Rose was dating Walter."

"It was just a cover. She's a lesbian and Walter told her not to let Jim know because he's a homophobe and so they started dating. But lately Walter's gotten kind of pushy."

"So Walter knows she's a lesbian?"

"Yes. So she says."

"Has she broken it off with him?"

"Not in so many words."

"So he doesn't know that the two of you are—"

Kelly turned furiously. "There's no way for him to know!"

"Maybe Rose told him."

"She wouldn't do that!"

"Why not?"

"She doesn't want to lose her job."

Dave crossed his arms over his chest. "I would have thought that she would be so angry at you coming in and usurping her position or, at least, potentially usurping her position that she would—"

"You know what, Dave?"

"What?"

"It was she who seduced me. Not the other way around."

"And you just went along—" Dave sneered.

"Fuck you. You have no right to judge me."

"You know what, Kelly?"

"What?"

"I think you should follow the advice in this note and watch out."

"Fuck you, Dave." She strode angrily toward the door.

"Kelly," he called after her, "I'm serious! Watch out!"

Her face was sullen when she turned back at the door to face him. "I still don't know if you did it." With that, she threw him a finger and walked out the door.

Once she was gone, Dave crumpled the scrap of paper in his fist and threw it viciously at the table, where it bounced and then skidded off the edge onto the wooden plank floor. He slammed his hands down on the table and leaned all of his weight against it.

"Christ," he said out loud. Deep in his gut, he felt a twist of fear accompanied by a vision of a failure. This caper, he perceived with prescient certainty, was not going to turn out as he had hoped.

By the time Rose got home from enlarging a clay figure of a

ELEVEN

bear totem at the foundry, Kelly was in quite a stew, if an inebriated one. Dave's accusation of Rose had tumbled repeatedly through her mind all afternoon and she had tried to think objectively about the matter.

Rose had a key to the house, Rose had access to her bedroom, Rose was...not mad at her. It didn't make sense. Besides what would Rose want her to watch out for? And if there was something she wanted her to watch out for, wouldn't she have just told her?

It was the same question she had asked Dave. The idea that Dave would do such a thing made very little sense even if she was disgruntled enough with him to think it possible he was covering up for his guilt by accusing Rose of the deed. Like Rose, if he wanted her to 'watch out', he would have just told her.

The destruction of Kitty's Pride was a warning of some kind, and not a very friendly one. Still, her mood was sour and her head hurt from thinking too much and drinking too much. When Rose walked in, Kelly was sitting at the kitchen table, her head down, her neck stiff, nursing her fifth beer.

"Hi!" Rose's greeting was cheerful, if tired.

"Hi, back," Kelly grumbled, not lifting her head.

"Hey," Rose went across to the kitchen sink to scrub the clay from her hands, "why so glum? And why are you hitting the bottle without me? Couldn't wait?" Rose's voice was teasing.

"Bad day."

Rose dried her hands. "The guys give you a hard time at the pour or what?"

"No. Check out my bedroom."

Rose frowned. "Your bedroom? What's wrong with your bedroom?"

Kelly glowered and nodded her head in the direction of the hall. "I was hoping you could tell me."

"I could tell you?" Rose hung back the towel and with a look hovering between curiosity and annoyance started down the hallway. Kelly got up and, gripping the beer by the bottle's neck, followed her.

"Holy shit," Rose exclaimed. "How did this happen?"

"I don't know. Do you know?"

"Why would I know?"

"Well, somebody— "

"You think I would break one of your pieces, Nancy?" Rose turned, her eyes piercing and angry. "Are you sure this isn't an accident?"

"It's not an accident. There was a note."

"A note? Where is it?"

Kelly searched her breast pockets. "Damn. I left it with Dave."

Rose frowned again but let the remark pass. "What did it say?"

"It said *watch out.*"

"'Watch out'? Who would be telling you to watch out? Watch out for what?"

"See, this is what I thought you might know."

"Might know what?" Rose's voice was rising.

"Might know who or what to watch out for. I mean who would give me a message like this? Who's pissed off at me?"

"How in the hell would I know?"

"You've been around the foundry longer."

"Oh, good heavens. That isn't very helpful." Rose shook her head. "I don't have a clue who might have done this or why."

"Oh, c'mon, Rose. Are you sure it wasn't you?" Kelly's voice was just a tiny bit slurred.

"Me!" Rose's eyes flashed. "You don't seriously mean that, Nancy, do you?

"I don't know." Kelly's eyes were big and sad and she was leaning against the door frame, her shoulders sagging.

"Oh, shit, girlfriend," Rose muttered. "You're not just upset over this, you're half-drunk. Now, I need to take a shower." Rose pushed past her, out of the bedroom.

Kelly turned and watched the other woman's departure, her head spinning at the sudden movement. "How do I know you didn't do it?"

"I didn't do it," Rose shouted, not looking back as she turned into the bathroom and slammed the door shut.

"Fine. Be that way!" Kelly likewise slammed her bedroom door and fell on to her bed, immune to the discomfort of akimbo segments of Kitty's Pride pushing up under her back.

"Who gives a fuck, anyway?" She asked out loud of no one and downed the last of her beer.

When Rose came to check on Nancy after taking her shower and eating a solitary dinner, she saw that Nancy was curled into a ball on top of her bedspread, snoring and clutching the empty longneck bottle against her torso. Rose gently pried the bottle from her fingers, careful not to wake her.

Piece by piece, Rose quietly dislodged the broken chunks of statuette from beneath Nancy's side and placed them in an empty box and stored them in the closet. She thought it was probably best if broken pottery was not the first thing Nancy saw in the morning.

Clearly, the wanton destruction—whatever the reason—had seriously upset Nancy. Rose didn't think Nancy had actually been accusing her of the deed: it was probably the beer talking.

Rose was sure Nancy would rush to apologize in the morning when she was sober. It hardly made sense that she would accuse her when their relationship was going along so smoothly and was so full of innocent joy.

When the bed was swept clear of pieces, she lifted the bedspread around the fully-clothed Nancy, tucking her beneath it as best she could, and tiptoed out of the room.

Rose went back to the kitchen, feeling a wave of loneliness wash over her. Even if it had only been a few weeks, she was now addicted to her and Nancy's evening chat over dinner and the wild passionate lovemaking that almost always followed.

Even if they didn't make love, they had taken to sleeping together which was something Rose truly enjoyed. It was still so early in their relationship, it was still fun to decide who's bed they would share each night: usually, it was a matter of how big a rush they were in to get each other's clothes off which determined where they ended up.

Rose was still hesitant to say—even to herself—that she was in love with Nancy and neither of them had said such words out loud except at the height of passion, something neither of them took too seriously. Of course, she said *I love you* at that moment—and so did Nancy—but what did it mean?

So far, Rose hadn't worried about it much. She was just enjoying the companionship, the exploring, the secret joys of having a lover and a friend, the relief at not having to pretend with Walter, although she didn't know yet how much he had guessed.

After that day in the foundry, she had avoided him and, for the moment, he seemed to be accepting the same cooling off period. Rose didn't know how long it would last: Walter had a persistent streak and she was sure matters were far from resolved. At some point, Walter would demand a 'yes-no' answer from her and probably a justification for breaking off their relationship.

She had spent far more time worrying about exactly how she was going to go about telling Walter that she didn't want his attentions, than she had spent wondering if Nancy was in love with her, or if she was in love with Nancy.

She certainly liked Nancy. The woman was attractive in a no-nonsense butch kind of way and intense about everything she did, including making love. It was clear she was determined to convince Jim she could run the foundry.

Rose didn't know if those qualities made Nancy the woman Rose was looking for but it did make her realize she didn't know a great deal about Nancy. She knew the luscious geography of Nancy's body and the way she thought about the foundry but what did she know about the woman herself? What did she know about her hopes and dreams? What did she know about her childhood, her past lovers, her views on nature, god and reality?

With all of their talking time taken up with the business of the foundry and all of their intimate time taken up with exercising their physical passion, neither one of them had talked much about their loves and hates, their pasts, or their goals. Rose suddenly realized she wanted to change all of that. She wanted to know and understand the real Nancy. If she didn't, how was she going to be able to decide if she loved the woman?

Rose smiled to herself as she turned out the lights in the kitchen and locked the front door. Beginning the next morning, she was going to start on the task of getting to know the real Nancy Summerhill.

She would start by helping Nancy sort through her feelings about the smashed piece and the supposed note. Rose didn't even know if Nancy was making up the part about the note. And, if there was a note, why had she shared it with Dave first, instead of with her? She knew Nancy and Dave were close because of Dave's long history with the family but, even so, it seemed odd that she had gone all the way into town to see him.

Had Nancy asked Dave if he had smashed Kitty's Pride? She would ask her tomorrow and they would have a full discussion of the matter. Rose brushed her teeth and grimaced at the hamper. Tonight should have been laundry night. They would have to make arrangements to go tomorrow instead. Rose put her toothbrush back in the bathroom cabinet and made her way to her bedroom.

After she got into the bed, she reached up to turn off the light. She couldn't imagine Dave smashing anything, let alone one of Nancy's pieces. He was just too sweet. Rose snuggled down under the covers, missing the languorous warmth of Nancy's body against her own. Damn it, but she hoped Nancy was in a better state of mind tomorrow. Why would anyone do something so adolescent as to smash someone else's property anyway?

In the next moment, Rose was asleep but in her dreams, a faceless man chased her across a dreary landscape of dead winter grass and leaf-naked trees, bearing aloft a bronze figure that she could never quite make out but which appeared to be a statue of two women entwined in a passionate embrace. If she slowed, the faceless man came near enough to swing at her with the bronze, and, frightened, she raced on.

The following morning, Saturday, Rose was awakened by her lover's head gently butting her between the shoulder blades.

"Grrrmn," Rose muttered, half-unconscious. "Stop it."

Kelly's arms went around Rose's shoulders and she pulled her snugly against her body. "I'm sorry," Kelly whispered into Rose's ear, followed by a warm tongue tickling at her ear lobe. Rose tried to shrug her off and snuggle back under the covers, her eyes still mutinously glued shut.

Kelly turned Rose in her arms and kissed her forehead and cheek and shut eyelids. "Hmmm," Rose murmured contentedly. She couldn't remember when someone had kissed her eyelids.

"Wake up, sleepyhead." Kelly blew hot air across her lips. "I'm taking you to breakfast and then we're hitting the great out-of-doors."

Rose's eyes came fully open. "Well, you're a lot more chipper than yesterday." She looked at her lover, who was already dressed in a long-sleeved denim shirt and jeans.

"That was yesterday. I'm not letting it get me down."

"Aren't you just a little bit hung over?"

"Nope. Threw up in the middle of the night, took some aspirin and now I'm fit as a fiddle. But I am starving." Kelly gave her lover a wolfish grin.

"All right then," Rose agreed, tossing off the covers. "I'll get showered and dressed. You can take me to Coyote Creek."

"Coyote Creek. Blue Corn." Kelly lolled back on the bed. "Doesn't anything have a normal name in this town like, say, Denny's or Village Inn?"

"Yeah, we've got those too but there not half as much fun. Besides, Coyote Creek is where all the hot-looking dykes go for breakfast on Saturday morning."

"Perfect!" Kelly crowed.

When they got there, the place did seem to be playing host to a preponderance of same-sex couples. Overall, the women were solid types who were wearing the kind of natural fabric clothes and cropped styles of hair that Kelly remembered from the Colorado gay community.

It was a cultural dynamic that said *we're take-charge, outdoors-women dykes: we can build a fire, replace the carburetor, break a horse, and still have time to meet you at noon to discuss politics or philosophy over a hamburger and a bowl of soup*. They were Kelly's favorite style of independent women.

"So, what did you conclude about yesterday's fiasco?" Rose had been watching Kelly as she appreciatively scanned the room and it reminded her of her thoughts from the previous day. How serious was she about Nancy and how serious was Nancy about her?

"Well," Kelly gulped foam off her tall glass of cafe latte and returned her attention to Rose, "you didn't do it and Dave didn't do it so I decided to forget about it and get on with my life."

"Do you think Walter did it?"

"It's possible." Kelly had not wanted to think too closely about Walter. "He does have a key to the house."

"Did he ever do anything like that when you were kids?"

"Uhh," Kelly hedged, "do you mean like destroy my stuff?"

"Yeah."

Kelly shook her head. "I can't remember. He was always trying to get my goat but if Walter did this, it seems like he's going a bit far."

"Has he said anything to you lately?"

"Not really. He told me to watch out yesterday during the pour."

"Watch out! Nancy! Duh!"

Kelly frowned, making the connection between the two incidents for the first time and then she discarded the notion. "That doesn't make any sense, Rose. He was just telling me to be careful because I lost my concentration for a minute."

"Maybe you really pissed him off and he thought you needed more of a warning or that you weren't taking him seriously. Spilling molten bronze on yourself could ruin your life, after all."

"I doubt he cares that much about me."

"Maybe not. But if you got hurt—if any of us got hurt—the foundry would have to pay out."

"Dave says Walter doesn't care about the foundry either." Kelly knew it was a mistake before the sentence was out of her mouth.

"Dave says...when did you talk to Dave about Walter?"

"Oh, it just came up one evening over dinner at Jim and Alice's. Besides, Rose, it's pretty obvious, isn't it? Walter didn't care about casting as a kid and he doesn't take a very active part in the business of the foundry even today except at pourings."

"True." Their orders arrived and they were temporarily distracted by plates heaped high with fluffy scrambled eggs, pan-fried herbed potatoes, thick bacon, and steaming green chile.

The meal was accompanied by a basket of Coyote Creek's speciality breads, scones, butter and raspberry jam.

"Where are we going today?" Rose asked when she was sated with food and coffee and people-watching.

"I was thinking Bandelier National Monument," Kelly said shyly. "I haven't been there in ages. In fact, I'm not sure I even remember how to get there!" She couldn't tell Rose she had spent 20 minutes very early that morning poring over the New Mexico highway map trying to locate it. She knew it was north of Santa Fe, near the once-secret city of Los Alamos where the atomic bomb that ended World War II had been developed.

"Don't worry. I can direct you. Bandelier has great hiking trails, too."

The road north incorporated some of the most stunning scenery Kelly had ever seen. Once they had climbed above the low-growing juniper trees and brilliant yellow scrub chamisa of the Espanola valley, the landscape was forested like Colorado except that cliffs of pink and yellow and white volcanic tuff towered along the roadway, forming interconnected mesas and canyons. The brilliant sunlight illuminating the crystal autumn air made the very rocks seem to come alive.

"This is breathtaking," Kelly said, having difficulty keeping her mind on the road and her eyes off the scenery.

Rose laughed. "Well, it hasn't changed in a few eons. I think the road might be newer than the one you probably remember."

Kelly reminded herself that she was supposed to have at least some familiarity with the locale. "Oh, you know how it is. When you're a kid you don't pay as much attention to the scenery. I just don't remember the road to Bandelier being this beautiful."

"I fell in love with it when I first came to New Mexico. I come up here as often as I can. It's a restorative for my soul...and my mind and my body."

Kelly laughed in relief. "Then you're going to know it a lot better than me so you can play tour guide."

"Okay. If you insist."

"When did you first come to New Mexico, Rose?"

"About six years ago. I was born in Pawhuska, Oklahoma which is Osage Indian country. So, Native American ways of thought were already familiar to me, even though the Osage are nothing like the Pueblo people here."

"Why did you move?"

"I wanted a career in sculpture and Santa Fe was always touted as the place. The thing is, you have to have money to make money in Santa Fe. It's hard to start at the bottom here, although I know of some people who have done it."

"I hadn't noticed that you've been casting any of your own works."

"I haven't. I got so absorbed in being the foundry manager, that my own creative well sort of dried up a bit. I'm not sure now if I'd rather be a manager than an artist and I was just fooling myself about sculpture."

"Somewhere in there is an artist, Rose. There always is."

"How did you know you were an artist? Was it just because you grew up in the foundry and you saw it happening every day around you?"

"No. It wasn't because of the foundry. In fact," Kelly knew she was inventing but she had to make her artificial past sound real, "I thought the foundry was keeping me from being an artist. I think the truth was I was afraid of the competition of 'real' artists, like the ones we work with at the foundry."

"I heard tell that you told your dad that you wanted to cast some of your own pieces."

"Yes, I do. I finally realized I was making my life harder than I needed to and I should just swallow my pride and come home." Internally, Kelly cringed. Yet there was a grain of truth in what she was saying. "I didn't want to go around to art fairs with my kiln-fired pieces forever. I wanted to make it. I wanted to do something of permanence. Why shouldn't I jump at the opportunity?"

Kelly wondered why she so desperately wanted Rose's blessing for her decision. It wasn't as if Rose knew what had really happened, anyway. If she did, she would almost certainly be horrified at Kelly's deception. So whatever blessing she gave now would be meaningless. Why did it matter anyway?

Rose shook her head. "There's no reason that I can think of that you shouldn't have come home. Particularly since it has been such a pleasure for me."

"Do you really mean that?" Kelly asked.

"Yes, I do. It's just that I don't know how you feel about it."

"The sex?"

Rose laughed. "No, not just the sex." Why were butches so dense, sometimes? she wondered. "The everything."

They were turning down a side road into Bandelier and, at the entrance station, Kelly yanked two five-dollar bills out of her wallet to pay the day use fee.

The road went across the mesa top for a short distance and then plunged down into Frijoles Canyon, which again took Kelly's breath away.

"Wow. This is some place!"

Kelly parked her truck amid the very old single story adobe buildings that formed the visitor center. Grabbing day packs and water bottles, they got out. A tiny stream, the Rito Frijoles, ran between golden cottonwoods along the canyon floor and birds of every description—pinon jays, robins, finches—called to each other.

Rose led the way past the buildings and along the trail that wound along the floor of the canyon before turning up into the volcanic tuff of the cliff side where naturally formed caves had been used as shelter by the earlier peoples who had lived in the canyon.

Although most visitors considered the caves and the ceremonial kivas the highlight of the monument, Kelly was in love with the small babbling stream and the golden cottonwoods, the warm sunlight, and the sense of utter peace and quiet that pervaded the canyon.

"It's easy to think of New Mexico as all deserts and cactuses," Rose remarked when they stopped along the trail for a breather, "but there are just as many high mountains and river canyons. That's why I fell in love with Bandelier when I first came to the state."

"It's idyllic," Kelly agreed. "And not a cactus in sight."

"If we hike down to the falls, we'll see plenty of cacti."

"Falls?"

"Yeah, waterfalls. There are two of them along the Rito Frijoles. From there, this stream drains into the Rio Grande but to get there you have to walk down a pretty steep trail between tall bluffs."

"I'm game. What about you?"

Rose looked up at the sky. "I think we could just make it down and back, but I don't know if we'd make it to the laundromat tonight."

"Ah, laundry, schmanundry. There's always tomorrow for laundry."

"Okay, just don't come crying to me if you don't have any underwear for tomorrow."

"Umm," Kelly leaned in close to tickle Rose's ear with her nose, and whispered, "wouldn't that create a bit of a diversion at the boring old laundromat?"

Rose grimaced and shrugged Nancy away. "That is the most unromantic venue I've ever heard of, Nancy Summerhill."

"When I was on the road, it was one of the only places to scout for girls. I had some pretty good times in laundromats."

"Clearly," Rose stood up and hauled Nancy to her feet, "your life has been lacking in sophistication."

"Which you're now going to provide, right?"

"Yes, but only if you answer the question I asked you earlier." Rose turned away from her and started hiking down the trail.

"What question was that?" Kelly hurried to catch up with her.

"How do you feel about us?"

"I feel great about us."

"You know what I mean."

"Oh, god. We're at that stage in our relationship where we have to start analyzing it." The trail had widened and they were able to walk along side by side.

"Well, that sounds a little negative, but I guess it's mostly true. Don't you feel a need to analyze it? I mean, where are we going with this?"

"Who cares? Let's just be here now."

"Nancy, don't you want to know a little bit more about me? I mean you didn't know enough about me yesterday to be able to make up your mind about whether I had smashed one of your pieces to smithereens. Don't you think that's important?"

"Oh, honey," Kelly took Rose's hand, "I was just upset."

"You weren't just upset, Nancy. You weren't sure."

"Aw, shit. It wasn't you. It was something Dave said that got my tail all twisted." The trail had narrowed again and begun to descend by switchbacks into Frijoles Canyon. Kelly was compelled to drop Rose's hand. She looked around and noticed they had lost track of the stream.

"What did Dave say?"

"He said since Kitty's Pride had been smashed on my bed that there was some hidden sexual meaning to that."

Rose couldn't look over her shoulder at Kelly because the trail was too steep and littered with shards of red rock that slipped along with their feet but she frowned anyway.

"Like what kind of sexual meaning?"

"I don't know. Like an ex-lover's revenge or something."

"We're not ex-lovers."

"Yeah, that's what I told him."

Rose screeched and Kelly leaped forward and grabbed her by the elbow. "Are you okay? Did you slip?"

Rose stopped her forward motion, which wasn't easy considering how one's body tended to succumb to the downward pull of gravity along the steep trail. Her knees and shins were already aching with trying to resist the pull.

"I didn't slip. Did you tell Dave we were lovers?"

"Yes. I mean, it was an accident, but yes, I did."

"Are you out of your mind? There goes my job for sure! Your dad's probably already put a pink slip in my mailbox!"

"No way, Rose! Dave isn't going to tell my dad."

Rose twined her middle and index fingers together. "Dave and your dad are like this."

"I know they're tight but he isn't going to tell Jim anything."

"What makes you so sure?"

"Umm, umm," Kelly searched Rose's beautiful hazel eyes, which at the moment were spitting fire at her, "Because Dave's gay himself."

"Dave's gay? You are a piece of work, Ms. Summerhill. That is the biggest bunch of bunk I've ever heard." Rose shook off Nancy's hold on her arm and started down the trail again.

Kelly was right behind her, but watching her feet, careful not to slip on the loose rocks. "You really didn't know that?"

"Why in hell would your dad put up with Dave all these years if he's as big an old homophobe as Walter claims?"

"Walter is full of shit!"

"Are you telling me Walter made that up about your dad?" They were nearly to the bottom of the switchbacks and Kelly could see the Rito Frijoles flowing along the floor of the canyon but she didn't see any waterfalls. Maybe the waterfalls were a come-on to entice people to hike down this rather treacherous, if stunningly beautiful, trail.

Rose was stamping across a log which traversed the stream as if she crossed it every day and then after a few more steps, turned off the trail toward a small pool. "What a disappointment," Kelly muttered, coming up behind Rose, who was pulling her boots off. "There's not a waterfall in sight."

"Boy," Rose said, stripping away her socks and settling her feet into the cold water, "you are unobservant."

"Oh, come on, there's no waterfalls around here."

Rose laughed. "Fifty feet back up the stream is the Upper Falls and right below this pool is the Lower Falls."

Kelly snorted and walked around to the edge of the pool. "Holy shit," she exclaimed, "there's a waterfall here!"

"Go up and see the other one," Rose commanded, "or you won't believe me."

"I believe you," Kelly asserted, tramping away up the stream.

When she returned, Rose had dried her feet and was in the process of retying her hiking boots. "Was it there?" Rose asked.

"It's still there." Kelly sat down beside Rose on the ground and was overwhelmed by her beauty. Why was this beautiful, intelligent woman hanging out with her, taking her hiking, sharing her bed? Kelly stretched out her legs and laid back, ignoring the sharp little rocks that dug into her back and pulled Rose down on top of her.

Kelly closed her eyes, fully concentrating on the warm moistness of Rose's lips, the pressure of Rose's breasts against her own, her dark hair falling forward to tantalize her and fill her nostrils with the musky odor of Rose's sandalwood shampoo.

"We will never get down to the Rio Grande and back at this rate," Rose reprimanded when they came up for air.

"Do we care?"

"No," Rose whispered. Their lips joined again and Rose's body swirled with desire. She settled her hips more firmly around Nancy's thighs and felt a warm pulse start between her legs. "Goddess," she murmured, "I thought I'd lost you."

"What do you mean?"

"Last night, Nancy. You were sure I'd violated your bedroom."

"There's no way you would do something like that."

"I know that, but you didn't know that."

Kelly sat up and pushed Rose away from her. "That's the second time you've said that today. What exactly are you getting at? I mean, I did apologize but if it's not enough..."

"It isn't that you didn't apologize. It's just that to me it means we don't know each other very well."

"Okay, granted. What do you suggest?"

"That we do exactly that."

"Exactly what?"

"Get to know each other better. You know, talk, share our pasts, discuss our plans for the future...that sort of thing."

Kelly swallowed hard. The word 'past' had riveted her attention on the real reason she was being so glib about Rose wanting to get to know her. She knew why she was refusing to look beyond the pleasure she was getting and giving in bed and why she couldn't form an honest relationship with Rose. Quite simply, she wasn't who Rose thought she was.

But how could she possibly tell Rose that?

Eppie's Laundromat featured the same scuffed linoleum floors, jimmied detergent dispenser, 'out of order' coin machine,

TWELVE

flickering florescent lights, and rows of battle-scarred washers that Kelly had encountered in every laundromat she had ever used. She wondered how long any of the equipment looked new and actually worked before it reached this expected, if depressing, state.

She dumped half of her bag of clothes, unsorted, into the nearest washer, ripped open a hand-sized box of detergent, emptied its shimmering blue-green granules into the mouth of the machine, and slammed closed the lid.

Wise in the ways of laundromats, she had brought a pocket full of quarters for the washers and dimes for the dryers. She laid four quarters in the aluminum slot arm and jammed the mechanism home. Her washer grunted to a start and she listened for the satisfying splash of water into the steel basin.

On the other side of the aisle, Rose sorted dark clothes from whites and dropped them into two side-by-side machines that were already churning with soapy detergent-laden water. Kelly repeated her actions at the next washer and then turned to Rose. "Are you almost done?"

"Almost."

"God, I'm tired and my feet ache." Kelly looked at her wristwatch. It was going on 11 p.m. and it had been a long day of hiking, an activity her muscles were not accustomed to. Her whole body was starting to stiffen up.

Crazily, they had hiked all the way down to the banks of the Rio Grande and only made it back to Kelly's pickup as the last shreds of the sunset faded in the west. They had driven back to Santa Fe, had dinner, and rushed to the modular to gather up their laundry.

"We can sleep in tomorrow," Rose said. "It's Sunday."

"Is that a promise?"

"We'll have to! We won't be home 'till one a.m. at this rate."

"Maybe we'll skip the dryers."

"Ugh. Wet clothes. I don't think so." Rose closed the lids of her two machines and came over to stand beside Nancy, who took her hand.

"Let's find a place to sit."

There was the usual row of molded plastic seats bolted to the floor facing a sheet of shiny darkness that, during the day, constituted the plate glass windows fronting the laundromat. Kelly could see their bodies reflected in the dark glass. This late on a Saturday night, the laundromat was deserted and all of the seats, except for theirs, were empty. They each settled into one and Kelly stretched her legs out in front of her, feeling pain grip her calves. She groaned.

"You're really sore," Rose said, looking at her with concern.

Kelly laid her head back against the thin rim of the molded seat, feeling it cut uncomfortably into her neck. "I'm out of shape.

For hiking, anyway."

"Better get in shape, woman. Next time, we're porting the canoe so we can go out on the rapids."

"Jeez, didn't you get enough adventure today?"

"Hardly." Rose grinned and leaned toward Nancy, planting a gentle kiss on her cheek. Her eyes softened with concern. "Why don't you take a hot bath when we get home?"

"I'd love to." Kelly closed her eyes. "If I don't fall asleep first. I guess I'm not as young as I used to be."

They both heard the swinging glass doors of the laundromat bang open. Rose glanced up and Kelly cocked open one eye. She sat up straight. Damn, if it wasn't Walter!

"So, ladies," he said, coming directly over, "you're out a bit late, aren't you?"

"Hi, Walter," Rose said carefully, "we went hiking and we got back late."

"Oh, yeah? Where'd you go?" He had come to a stop and towered over them, his eyes keen with interest.

"Bandelier," Kelly answered. "We hiked down to the Rio."

Walter's eyebrows quirked upwards. "You don't say."

"Why are you here, Walter?" Rose asked. "I thought you had a washer/dryer at your apartment complex."

"I'm not here to do laundry." He looked from one to the other of them and then settled his attention on Rose. "I'm here to talk to you, Rose."

"At 10:30 at night?"

"I expected you to be available to go out tonight. I hung around and waited for you."

Color flushed into Rose's cheeks. "We didn't have any official plans, Walter."

"I think you've been avoiding me." His jaw was set, the brightness in his eyes darkening to menace.

Kelly stood. "You know what, Walter. You're right. She is avoiding you."

"Nancy," Rose stood up and put a restraining hand on Nancy's arm, "it's okay. Let's not start a fight here."

"No," Walter replied, his hand rising to block Rose, "let's hear what my dear sister has to say."

Kelly sighed in exasperation. "Look, she wants you to leave her alone. That's enough, Walter. There's nothing else to say."

"I think," Walter threatened, "there's a lot more to say, or at least, to ask. Are you breaking up with me, Rose?"

Rose dropped her head and scuffed her dusty boots against the floor.

"Yes."

"Are you hanging out with my sister now?"

"Yes."

Walter's eyes narrowed so much his face scrunched into a hard knot of anger. "That is disgusting," he spit out. "You are both disgusting. You are despicable and disgusting!"

"You are disgusting, Walter!" Rose shouted back. "Just keep away from me!"

Walter ignored her and turned his attention to Kelly. Feeling like a moth pinned to a board, she felt the intensity of his anger burn its way through her chest, leaving a chill of fear lingering in its wake. When he spoke, his tone was guttural, like the growl of an offended animal. "Don't think for one second, *Nancy*, that you can get the foundry away from me."

He turned and strode toward the entrance of the laundromat, slamming the glass doors open with his clenched fists on the way out and disappearing instantly into the darkness of the night.

"Shit!" Rose howled, "shit!" She started to shake and turned to bury her head against Nancy's chest. Automatically, Kelly slipped her arms around Rose's trembling frame but, internally, she felt nothing but the numbness of shock. For the first time, Walter had called her 'Nancy'. Why now?

The next morning, after Kelly awoke and viewed the tousled sweetness of her sleeping lover, she decided she wanted to surprise Rose with bagels and lox and cream cheese and the best coffee she could find for breakfast.

She'd have to go out and buy these goodies, of course, but she was sure the nearby grocery store opened just as early on Sunday as any other day. Easing stealthily out of bed, she slipped on her jeans and a t-shirt and let herself out of the house.

On the deck outside the door, she stopped and looked around, drawing in the still bright air of the autumn Sunday. The foundry parking lot was deserted and there was no one about. Kelly stepped forward—not looking down—and tripped, flying straight over both steps and landing hard on the gravel of the parking lot on her knees.

Instinctively, she rolled and because she was still, in her mind, acting stealthily so she wouldn't wake Rose, she didn't cry out. Instead, she laid on her back on the ground, gripping her knees and cursing under her breath. She rolled from side to side, her teeth gritted, until the pain started to subside.

"Shit, shit, shit!" she finally muttered, sitting up and rubbing the knee that hurt the most. It was going to show one hell of a bruise. She hoped that was all and that she hadn't actually damaged her knee. Tentatively, she stretched out her leg and felt pain twang in all directions but nothing that took her breath away.

Slowly, she got to her feet, putting her weight on the leg that only felt jarred and bruised and then transferred it, little by little, to the leg with the injured knee. It took her weight without any frightening pains rushing up and down her leg.

Now that she was upright and her greatest worry was over, other parts of her body started to scream in protest. In particular, her scraped palms throbbed and burned. She examined her palms and brushed gravel from the wounds. Her shoulders felt jarred and she was sure they would be sore for a few days.

She took a step forward, exercising care with her leg. God, it hurt! She looked back toward the modular, wondering longingly about going in immediately and icing it but machismo finally won out. She wanted desperately to surprise Rose.

She limped to her truck, dragged herself aboard and headed for the grocery store, thankful it wasn't her clutch-operating leg that was hurt. She didn't think she could have endured that much knee action. Fifteen minutes into her rounds at the store, she realized she'd made a big mistake not icing the leg. For one thing, her knee was swelling and for another, her awareness of her overall pain was increasing.

She had the basics of bagels and cream cheese and lox in hand, though. They would have to make do with regular non-designer coffee. A bit breathless from the pain, but maintaining a cheerful, everything-is-fine front, she checked out with her purchases.

She climbed back into her truck and latched her seat belt, gritting her teeth. She had failed to buy aspirin but she wasn't going back into the store. She would have to wait until she got home. How could she have been so damn clumsy, anyway?

Kelly turned onto Airport Road a few minutes later and breathed a sigh of relief at her nearness to home. The four-lane road was mostly deserted so early on a Sunday morning and, in what she considered a well-justified hurry, she pushed her truck into fourth gear and sped up a bit over the 35 mile per hour speed limit.

Less than a quarter mile from the entrance to the foundry, the steering wheel wrenched itself from Kelly's scraped and burning hands and the truck swerved wildly out of control, heading off the roadway toward a telephone pole. The last thing Kelly consciously remembered was applying the brakes, which didn't seem to slow her much.

She didn't remember the front end of the truck scraping the pole, whipping the body of it around 360 degrees and tightly wrapping the bed of the truck against its splintered column, like a predator claiming its prey. Nor did she consciously hear any of the ugly, screeching, crushing noises that went with this process, including the final eerie thud that defined the end.

The first noise she acknowledged and wondered about was the sound of sirens. Looking up from where her head rested against the steering wheel and out over the strangely tilted hood of her truck, she saw flashing lights.

The lights made her feel dizzy and she put her head back down. She was aware that there were people standing outside the door of her truck cab because she could hear them. When she next looked up again, she could see their panicked faces.

There was something sticky on her mouth that tasted bitter and a horrendous pain in her knee. The people standing outside her window took form as a woman and two men in police officers' uniforms. One of the men was trying to open her cab door but it seemed to be jammed. For the first time, she noticed the cab window had been shattered into a dazzling array of rectangular bits of glass held together by an inner lining of what looked like blue Saran Wrap. Smart invention, she thought disconnectedly.

She wondered where Rose was and if she would still want the bagels when Kelly got home. Suddenly, without any warning to herself and apparent cause as near as she could muddle out, she started to bawl. She could feel the tears running down her cheeks and mixing their saltiness with the other, unidentified bitter taste on her lips.

She raised her hands and felt pain shoot unexpectedly through her shoulders. She laid her elbows against the steering wheel and rested her head there. She felt very confused and very tired which didn't make sense to her because it was early morning and she knew she'd gotten a full night's sleep. Still, her head was starting to hurt and she missed Rose. Where was Rose?

Kelly heard a high whine to her right and turned her head to look. There were more people standing on that side of her truck. They were backing away and one man, carrying a tool she didn't recognize, stepped forward. The unidentified tool disappeared from Kelly's view and so did her interest in whatever mysterious activity the man was undertaking.

It seemed like only a moment later when she felt a cool breeze against her side and there was another man sitting next to her on the old torn seat of her truck. She felt embarrassed, and violated too, because he had stepped right on top of the bagels and cream cheese and lox, which curiously, had fallen to the floor.

The man was smiling and talking to her but she didn't feel like responding. Her head was too heavy. When he touched her shoulder, she lifted her head up and looked straight out the windshield. The windshield, at least, was as she remembered it: cracked, pitted and streaked with irreparable scratches from bad wiper blades.

"Look," she said, lifting her aching arm to point at a slight dark-haired person running up the roadway toward the truck, "there's Rose." Kelly felt a sudden indefinable sense of relief.

"She loves me after all."

"Good," soothed the man, "you're talking."

Kelly put her head back down on the steering wheel and felt a swirl of blackness. "She loves me," she repeated in a whisper, not for the man's benefit but solely for hers. The blackness swirled again. It was sweet and seductive like Rose's hair: it passed over her closed eyes and gently carried her into oblivion.

When Kelly next woke up, Dave was sitting beside her, holding her hand. She was flat on her back in a strange bed and she struggled immediately to sit up. Dave eased her back down.

"Calm down," he said. "You're in the hospital."

"Where's Rose?" She demanded, her voice near tears. "Where are the bagels?"

Dave smiled. "Rose is here. She just stepped into the bathroom. I don't know where the bagels are."

Tears started to flow down Kelly's cheeks.

"Oh, thank goddess! You're awake!" Rose appeared on the other side of her bedside and Kelly twisted her head to look at her. "Oh, god, honey," the words flowed unbidden out of Kelly. "I'm so sorry. I was bringing you bagels and I don't know what happened to them."

"Oh, sweetheart," Rose said, leaning down to wipe away Nancy's tears with her fingers, "it's okay. Don't worry about the bagels."

"I wanted to surprise you for breakfast. There was cream cheese and lox, too."

Rose gave Dave a meaningful glance and he stood up and moved away from the bed. Rose took Nancy's hand and leaned close to her.

"You are the most thoughtful lover," she whispered, her voice an intimate caress, "sneaking out to get me breakfast like that. As soon as you're better, we'll go out and have all the bagels and cream cheese and lox we want. We'll go wherever you want to go."

"I don't care where we go. I just want to be with you." Kelly knew she sounded peevish, like a child, and she couldn't understand why she felt so frustrated.

"I'm right here with you," Rose reassured. "Why don't you rest again, now?"

"Okay." Kelly did feel inordinately tired but she didn't know why. She felt like she'd been sleeping forever.

The next time she woke up, Kelly was mentally clearer. She was aware she was in the hospital and recollected she'd been in an accident, but she didn't remember anything about the accident itself.

She was also ravenously hungry. It was 2 a.m. on Monday morning, but Kelly didn't know that or that the food service in the hospital was closed for the night.

"There's a lot more color in your cheeks," Rose said when Nancy's eyes fluttered open.

"Hi," she said.

"How do you feel?"

"I'm starving."

Rose laughed. "That's my girl!"

"Am I allowed to have something to eat?"

"Yes. Definitely. What do you want?"

"A hamburger with all the fixings."

"Fries? Malt? Soda?"

"No fries. A chocolate malt would be awesome."

Rose stood up and cocked a pose, pretending to write on a non-existent order pad. "That'll be $3.49, miss," she teased.

"I love you," Kelly said.

"I'll have to find an open burger place, so it will be a few minutes, baby." She leaned down to kiss Nancy on the cheek. "However, you should be in good hands with Dave, here."

"What is he, Allstate or something?"

"Thank god, you are better, Nancy."

Kelly waited until Rose was gone from the room and then she turned to Dave. "What in the hell happened?"

"I was going to ask you the same question. Do you remember anything?" There was a worried look in Dave's bright eyes.

"Don't worry. I remember the whole Nancy charade. I don't remember anything beyond getting bagels for breakfast. I was in a hurry to get home to Rose, but I'm not sure why. Did someone hit me?"

Dave shook his head, looking somber. "You hit a telephone pole. The police think you were traveling a little above the speed limit but you weren't going excessively fast. Not so fast that you should have lost control."

"I hit a telephone pole?" Kelly's stomach turned over and her face blanched.

"Hey," Dave soothed. "I'm sorry. I thought you were ready to talk about it or you wouldn't have asked."

Kelly flapped her hand against the sheet and swallowed hard. "It's okay. It's just that my mom always told me that my biological mom was killed in a collision with a telephone pole in Trinidad, Colorado. I was just a few months old at the time."

"That's awful, Kelly. Is that why you were adopted?"

"No. My birth mom gave me up for adoption at birth. I was already living with my adopted parents at the time she was killed. When I was about 14 years old and started asking questions, my adopted mom told me my biological mom had been killed in an auto accident. I never questioned it. I just assumed it was true."

"I'm sure it is."

Kelly twisted her head against the pillow to look at Dave. "How's my truck?"

"Totaled."

"Shit, Dave. I loved that truck. That truck was my whole life." Tears formed in Kelly's eyes. She wiped them away with her fist. "Well, it used to be anyway."

"Do you remember anything, Kelly? Something running in front of you? Something distracting you?"

Kelly pondered until her head hurt. "Nothing. I can't remember anything."

"Memory is tricky and the doctor said that sometimes you won't remember what happened. But it may come back to you later. Still, the paramedics couldn't figure out how your knee got swollen because it wasn't touching the frame of the truck or how your hands got scraped. It didn't look like those injuries happened in the accident. Do you remember anything about that?"

Kelly laughed. "Oh, yeah! I do remember that! I was being a total klutz. I tripped coming out of the modular and I landed on my hands and knees."

Dave frowned. "What did you trip on? Was there something on the porch you didn't see?" Had something happened to Kelly's eyesight or her reflexes that could explain both accidents?

"No. I just tripped. Next thing I knew I was flying through the air. Then I was on the gravel. Man, it hurt but I didn't want to wake Rose so I didn't even howl."

"And you just went on to the grocery store for the bagels?"

"Okay, so I was being a bit macho, Dave. Sometimes you're not in that much pain right away."

Dave shook his head. "You are too much!"

"Oh," Kelly exclaimed, "that's why I was in a rush to get home! I limped around the grocery store and by then my knee was starting to hurt real bad and I knew I needed to ice it. It's not busted, is it?"

"They took an x-ray and, no, they don't think so. They figure you have a concussion, though, because your head hit the steering wheel and you've been out for quite a long time. You have a bump on your forehead, which bled a lot, and they said your chest and abdomen were bruised from the seat belt."

Kelly reached up to touch the bump on her forehead. It felt uncomfortable and she dropped her hand.

"Actually, considering the shape the truck was in and that they had to cut you out of it, you sustained very few serious injuries."

"Thank god for seat belts," Kelly agreed.

"Well, you're not out of the woods, yet. You'll have to take it easy for awhile because some injuries don't show up right away." Dave's expression was worried.

"Meaning?"

He tried his most reassuring smile. "Meaning Jim isn't going to let you work until you have a doctor's release."

"Oh, shit. I have those two commissions to finish!"

"Kelly—"

"How is the old guy, by the way?"

"You scared the holy hell out of him. You are his great white hope, you know."

"Did he come by to visit?"

Dave shook his head. "Sorry. Understandably, he hates hospitals. He sure cares about you though. He's going shopping for a new truck for you."

"A new truck! Is he out of his mind? He can't do that."

"Well, I think he's going to let you make the final decision but you know how insistent he can be."

Kelly started to giggle. "Where has this man been all my life?"

Dave joined in her laughter. "There's nothing like a sugar daddy. I wish I could find one!"

"You will, Dave. Don't worry. You will."

By noon on Monday, Kelly had been released from the hos-

THIRTEEN

pital. She limped out, a soft cast on her knee, a large swath of bandage on her forehead and her weight on Dave's and Rose's arms. She spent the next few days either sleeping or in the kitchen of the modular, sitting at the table and molding in clay. Rose insisted on fixing every meal and checking on her every few hours.

"You know, Rose," Kelly said on the morning of the third day, while Rose made poached eggs for breakfast, "I wish you'd stop worrying. I'm going to be fine. You've really been fretting over me. Not that I'm not flattered, but—"

"Sometimes negative aftereffects don't show up until later, Nancy."

"I've heard that too, but I feel fine. You know, the doctor said I'd be fine."

"I know, but she's not in love with you the way I am." Rose slid the eggs onto plates and sat down at the table and looked as if she was going to start to cry.

"Baby," Kelly said, "you know what you need?"

"You mean," Rose sniffled, "other than a good roll in the hay?"

"Yes," Kelly laughed. "Other than that. Give me a few more days on that one. My ribs are still real sore. Let's go somewhere. The weather is beautiful for so late in the year."

"Actually, funny you should mention that. Last night, Walter invited me to go sailing on Cochiti Lake today. He's taking his catamaran out."

"What did you say?"

"I said hell no. But if you want to go, that would be different. You wouldn't have to do anything except lay on the deck and enjoy the sunshine. Walter's really been pleasant the last few days. I think he's worried about you."

"Sounds nice, actually. I've never been sailing."

Rose frowned. "I thought you and Walter used to sail all the time."

Kelly shook her head and the movement made it hurt. "I didn't mean never. I meant since I left home."

"See what I mean? It's those concussion aftereffects."

"You're probably right." Kelly's stomach was tight. Maybe the concussion had affected her more than she realized. She was going to have to be careful. Rose might not notice a lapse but Walter certainly would.

"If you're not up to it—"

"No. Call Walter. Let's go. It will be good for all of us, I'm sure."

The leaves of the massive cottonwoods in the Rio Grande

river valley were the perfect yellow-gold of late October that photographers waited for all year and the sky arching overhead was a perfect eggshell blue. The few clouds that drifted past were high feathery wisps of white, hinting at winter.

There was a breeze but it was light, just enough to stir the cottonwoods and blow aloft the smoke that rose from the pudgy-shaped outdoor bread baking ovens, or *hornos,* at Cochiti Pueblo. It helped the catamaran glide across the open mesa-flanked bowl of the lake toward the river's gorge, the *Caja del Rio.*

"This is quite a treat," Walter remarked for the second time, "having both you gals out here when all I was expecting was a solitary day on the lake."

"It's a lovely day and we appreciate the invitation," Rose said, accommodating Walter in order to maintain what she saw as a fragile peace. She was still feeling skittish about their encounter in the laundromat but Walter acted as if he'd forgotten the incident.

"Hey, no problem. My sis sure needed to get out of the house. I know her well enough to know she was starting to get cabin fever. How's that bump on your head feeling, Nancy?"

"It's there," Kelly answered, her sunglass-clad eyes following the lazy drift of the clouds. "This sure is relaxing though, Walter."

"Yeah, I love to sail. Did you sail while you were away, Nancy?"

"No. Never got a chance."

Walter was sitting cross-legged on the deck, on the opposite side of the sail from the women, sipping a beer. He was dressed in shorts, t-shirt, denim bill cap, and a bright orange safety vest.

The sail was perfectly attuned to the wind and the catamaran skipped pleasantly along—not too fast and not too slow. His ship properly rigged for the moment, Walter turned his head to look at Rose. "Nancy was big into sailing when we were teenagers. We were out here all the time."

"Why do you like to sail, Walter?" Rose asked.

"Well, you can see that pretty easy. It's fun. It's an escape. It's just you and the boat and the water. No bosses, no rules, no paperwork. I like that." He took a draught off his beer bottle.

"Why Cochiti?"

Walter grinned, his eye teeth showing. "It's close to home. Truth is, being a man-made lake, it just looks like a giant toilet bowl. Advantage is you can see everything and it's easy to maneuver a boat around in."

"Oh, give me a break," Kelly said. "It's beautiful the way the Jemez Mountains rise behind the mesas. You like it better than that, Walter. It's sure always been one of my favorite places." Kelly had put the statement into the past but she was, in fact, fast falling in love with the desert beauty around her.

"No," he shrugged. "I've just learned to make do with it. Hey, Nanc, do you remember that day we were out here and you lost..." Walter paused.

"Lost what?" Rose intervened, sure this was another of Walter's weird tests of his sister's memory.

Walter ignored Rose. "Do you remember?" The teasing look in his eyes had developed that strange glint that Rose was beginning to notice more frequently with Walter. She thought the relaxed stance of his elbows resting on his knees had tightened. He took a sip of his beer.

Kelly rolled languidly onto her side to face him. "Do you mean my jade necklace?"

Beer spurted from Walter's mouth and he shot to his feet and pounded his chest. Kelly smiled inwardly, grateful Dave had told her the apparently inconsequential story of the loss of a necklace special to Nancy because Barbara had given it to her and Walter had questioned its origin.

Unlike the other tests, the jade necklace story had to be an identity clincher for Walter because only Walter and Nancy had been aboard the catamaran when the necklace fell into the lake. Walter would now be at a loss to explain how Kelly, as the interloper he seemed so convinced she was, could possibly recall an event only he and Nancy had shared.

"Are you okay?" Rose bobbed to her feet and Kelly found herself admiring her lover's round firm buttocks, made even more pert by the short shorts she was wearing. Definitely, Kelly was feeling better. Maybe even tonight she could do something about her perking hormones.

"I just swallowed my beer wrong," Walter explained, waving off Rose's solicitude. Although the bottle was only half-empty, he tossed it into the lake with a vigorous gesture of dismissal. "Gotta stop drinking that stuff anyway." His face was a mask of glowering anger.

Rose backed away from him and sat down beside Nancy, her forehead creased in a frown. Walter began to fiddle with the ropes, ignoring the women. Rose looked quizzically at Nancy.

"Beats me," Kelly whispered. "Don't worry about it." She put her arm around her lover's waist, below the bulky foam of Rose's life vest. "Just enjoy the beauty of the day with me."

"Okay." They sailed in silence for a while, surrounded by the silver-blue of the lake's face, the piercing blue of the sky, and the maroon and tan of the nearby lava-encrusted mesas. Kelly felt remarkably at peace. Her life, despite the accident, was looking up.

She had a lover, she had a job, she was luxuriating in this brand new experience of sailing, and soon she would have a new truck. Jim, accompanied by Dave, had brought her a stack of glossy brochures the previous day from all the major truck dealers and asked her to compare features and prices.

"You can't buy me a truck," she had protested to Jim.

"I'm not going to," he replied. "I'm just going to put up the down payment and co-sign the note, because you don't have any credit. Alice will deduct the payment directly from your bi-weekly check so you don't have to think about it."

"You'll need to take a percentage of the down payment and interest out of each check, too," she insisted.

"Hell, no," he told her. "Also, I'm giving you a $200 a month raise to offset the cost of the truck."

"Dad! You can't give me a raise. I haven't even finished my first two commissions! You can't give me a raise until I bring in some serious business to the foundry."

"If I want to give you a raise, young lady, I'll give you a raise."

"Dad," she remonstrated, "the foundry can't handle it! Things are too tight right now." In the end, they compromised on a $100 raise but Jim Summerhill would hear nothing about her paying back the $2000 down payment he was going to make on her behalf.

All in all, Kelly thought dreamily, things were going very well. The only sound was the hum of the breeze striking the sail and the slap-slap of the twin hulls of the catamaran as they rode the gentle swells. Rose's back pushed up against her belly where Kelly lay on her side and Kelly, her arm wrapped around her lover's middle, felt a deep contentment. So deep a contentment, that she soon fell asleep.

Waking up was a cold wet shock and it was only instinctual that she was holding her breath as she flailed her limbs beneath the water of the lake. A long moment passed while, lungs bursting, she peered befuddled through layers of muddy water, not knowing where the surface of the lake lay.

An instant later, the buoyancy of her life vest shot her upward and she broke the cold surface, gasping for air. She moved without thought toward one of the upturned hulls of the catamaran, but the hull shifted away from her as the aluminum struts of the sail bobbed to the surface and the catamaran heaved onto its side, one hull lifting out of the water.

"Jesus Christ!" she sputtered, spitting muddy water from her mouth and still struggling to get a deep breath. "What in the hell happened?" She swam around toward the listing sail infinitely grateful for the life vest but madder than a drowned rat, which, at the moment was what she was.

Walter, his head visible above the sail, his body bobbing in the water, shouted, "She capsized!" His eyes were bright and his mouth was locked in a grin.

"Capsized? How?" Kelly screamed back. "And where's Rose?"

"Here," Rose called, dog-paddling toward them.

"Can you swim?" Kelly shouted.

"Yes. I'm fine. It's just when I saw the hulls go under the water I couldn't believe it."

"Walter," Kelly turned her attention back to the man who was heading this expedition, "what in the hell happened?"

"Rose is right. The hulls went under. Shit! I think I know what happened." Walter swam around toward the rear of the hulls and examined them.

"What is it?" Kelly shouted, starting to shiver. It might be a warm pleasant day in late October but lake water in New Mexico was notoriously cold at any time of the year. Not somewhere to spend a lot of time without a wetsuit for protection.

"I forgot to put the plugs back on the hulls. I was working on the cat last week. It looks like the hulls filled up with water. That's what took her down."

"You forgot to put the plugs back!" Kelly could feel steam coming out of her ears. "How in the hell does that constitute being sure your equipment is shipshape! You are such an asshole, Walter."

"Well," he answered, his expression unreadable but not, she thought, particularly perturbed, "nothing to do about it now."

Rose called out: "It's getting damn cold in this water, Walter. What are we going to do?"

Walter looked around, eyeing the distance to the vast rocky bulk of Cochiti Dam and the more distant docking shore. Both were very far away for swimmers who weren't in Olympic shape. "We're going to have to right the cat," he answered, turning back to look at the two women.

"Are you out of your mind?" Kelly's teeth were chattering.

"What choice do we have?" He gestured toward the looming, but distant, dam, encouraging her to make her own assessment.

"All right," Kelly grumbled. "What do you want us to do?"

"If all three of us climb onto the hull that's out of the water at the same time, I think we'll have enough combined weight to bring the sail up."

Together, they swam behind the catamaran and on Walter's count of three raised their arms to the hull. Kelly found it impossible to pull her wet weight from the water so she just hung from the hull, hoping it would make a difference.

Walter, being taller and heavier, was already scrambling onto the hull and his weight was forcing it to teeter back toward the surface of the lake. As it fell toward the water, both women clambered on. The wet sail rose, spraying them with the water that had collected on its surface, and Rose heaved a huge sigh of relief.

Everything that had been aboard the flat open deck of the

catamaran had been swept into the lake and was no more: the cooler, their jackets, and the loose ropes. The hats and sunglasses they had been wearing had been lost when the threesome tumbled into the water.

Kelly laid in a ball on the damp deck and shivered, praying for more solar wattage from the October sun, anything to still the chattering of her teeth and ease the tight pain in her stomach. There were no dry clothes to change into or anything else to wrap herself in to avoid loss of body heat.

"I'm sorry I can't do all that much to keep you warm, honey," Rose murmured, anxiety marking her voice. "You don't need any more trauma. This wasn't supposed to happen."

"That damn Walter," Kelly replied between gritted teeth. "Of all the stupid things. He should know better! How could anyone do anything so plain out stupid! And he prides himself a sailor! We could have all been killed!"

Rose couldn't tell if Walter was catching Nancy's verbal castigation because he was busily resetting the sail to catch the breeze to take them back to shore.

"I think there are some beach towels in my truck," Walter said once the sails were set and the catamaran had chugged to a bumpy start. "You can dry off when you get there." The catamaran, heavy with the load of water in its hulls, moved at a dead slow pace through the water, but it did move toward shore. "Until then, just think warm thoughts."

Taking his words beyond thought to action, Rose wrapped her body around Nancy's and held her tightly, both of them dripping cold water onto the deck. The heat from the autumn sun was offset by the breeze that rushed steadily over their wet uncovered heads.

When they reached the shore, Kelly was so stiff she could hardly move. Rose demanded Walter's truck keys—which, he hadn't carried with him but instead were hidden in a magnetic keyholder inside the left front fender of the truck. He told her where the keys were and she hustled Kelly into the cab. The truck had been parked facing the sun so the interior was hot.

"Oh, this is heavenly," Rose exclaimed as she jumped onto the wide red vinyl seat and stripped off her wet clothing. When she was naked, she helped the more hypothermic and slower-moving Nancy strip off hers. Together, they breathed in the heat of the cab like a fine perfume. Freed from the cold weight of her wet clothes, Kelly felt the heat soaking into her skin and she melted with sheer physical gratitude.

"I'm never going to complain about my truck cab getting too hot in the summer ever again," Rose said. She searched for the towels stashed behind the seat and, bringing up two, handed one to Nancy.

"Are you recovering?" Rose asked.

"My teeth aren't chattering any more. I was starting to feel incoherent. I didn't know if I would be able to talk." The sentences came out in choppy phrases. "I don't know when I was last so cold. I'm getting warmer now. I was scared."

"I think you're going to be okay, sweetheart." Rose kissed her on the cheek in reassurance. There was a rap at the window and they both looked up. It was a naked Walter, gesturing for a towel. Rose dug behind the seat and came up with another towel which she handed out to him.

After drying off, Walter, his teeth still chattering and the towel strapped around his waist, climbed into the driver's seat.

"At least it's toasty warm in here. Are you two better?" He warily eyed them. They were wrapped from breast to thigh in large thick beach towels and neither looked particularly friendly.

"I loaded the cat myself," he pronounced, turning over the key in the ignition, "so we can just head on home." Walter's feet were bare and he grunted as he pressed down the clutch with his unprotected foot.

"Sorry about that," he apologized as his Dodge Ram climbed up the long loading ramp from the lake to the main roadway.

"Walter," Kelly said, "I'm not even speaking to you so don't try to talk to me."

"Rose?"

"Same here."

It was, therefore, an exceedingly silent ride back to the foundry except for the blast of oldies from the radio which Walter finally, in desperation, turned on.

Kelly was awakened in the night by a nightmare featuring a

FOURTEEN

giant wave, the size of a tsunami. The wave, towering so tall over her head as to block out the sun, waited very politely to rush in and destroy everything on land for miles around, while she sat on the beach and played a single game of four-sided chess—an impossible game her imagination had devised—with Walter and Jim and Dave and Rose.

Of the five players, she seemed to be the only one aware that a tsunami was inches away. She knew, when she got to the end of the game, the wave would break and fall, killing all of them. Yet, despite her knowledge of impending disaster, the game drew inexorably to a close and she could do nothing to prevent it. When it looked like Walter would checkmate her, she begged him not to, to suspend time by leaving the game as it stood, to run or to let her run.

Ignoring her pleas, he smiled maniacally at her and pronounced, "Checkmate, sis." At that moment, the wave fell, its vast blue-green force pounding on her skull and stealing the breath from her lungs. She was tossed by the wave, so crushed and battered, she could no longer think or breathe.

Kelly forced herself upright in the bed gasping for air, tears spilling from the corners of her eyes. The muscles of her arms were trembling. "Shit," she mumbled and coughed. Mucus came up with the cough and she realized she must have swallowed bacteria-laden lake water.

Her sinuses ached, her throat burned, and her muscles felt stiff. Damn it! She was probably coming down with a cold. Of course, after everything she'd been through, it was hardly surprising.

She shuffled into the bathroom and turned on the shower as hot as she could stand it. After the water had heated her muscles, she swathed herself in her only pair of heavy knit sweatpants and sweatshirt and trudged into the kitchen, switching on the small task light over the stove.

The digital clock on the microwave read 2:31. She put the kettle on the gas and got honey and rum from the cabinet and a fresh lemon from the refrigerator. The warm sweetness of the drink felt good on her throat and the rum vapors wafted up into her nose. As she sipped at her version of the classic hot toddy, her mind idled over the events of the last few days. Way too much had happened: she had taken a hard fall, her truck had been totaled, her head concussed, and her body dumped in a cold lake.

How could Walter have been so stupid? She still couldn't find an answer to that question. What right-thinking sailor—and Walter sailed on a regular basis and had been doing so for years—didn't put the plugs back into the hulls of his catamaran? What right-thinking sailor even removed the plugs? What were the plugs there for?

Kelly didn't know enough about catamarans to know the answer and had no idea who she could ask. Still, it seemed like an incredibly egregious oversight. It would be like taking out a road bike without checking the brakes.

The brakes. Kelly experienced a sudden drop in her stomach. She had a dim recollection of her foot touching brakes but she couldn't place the event in time. Brakes, brakes, why was that important?

She felt a sudden wrenching pain in her shoulders and winced. Where had that come from? An even vaguer image of her hands holding something in front of her came to her mind but she couldn't place the scene.

Kelly shook away the unsubstantial cobwebs of her memory and took another sip of her drink. Her mind circled back to Walter.

He was so strange, she thought, so hard to figure. Hot and cold by turns, almost erratic. For one thing, if he hadn't accommodated himself to her and Rose's relationship, then why had he invited them out for a sail?

Of course, he hadn't really invited her. Maybe he had just wanted to take another crack at developing a relationship with Rose. Which didn't make sense either since it seemed pretty clear that Rose wasn't interested. Still, guys could be very persistent.

And, if he'd given up on the relationship with Rose, why hadn't he gotten a thwarted lover's revenge and reported Rose's 'perversion' to Jim? Even worse, let Jim know she was carrying on this perversion with Jim's daughter. That could easily land both her and Rose in the street. There would be no new truck and no new raise then.

What Walter had said to her in the foundry and what he had said to them both in the laundromat was hard to forget and hard to dismiss. On the other hand, Walter almost seemed to have forgotten it. Did people just sweep aside their homophobia to achieve other objectives? If so, what were his other objectives?

Kelly fiddled the mug nervously between her fingers. Why hadn't Walter pushed his advantage? Especially as regarded Kelly, he had tremendous cards to play and the motivation to play them. It was clear to her, even with her talent for throwing him off his guard, that he did not believe she was Nancy. And if he was so sure she wasn't Nancy, why hadn't he said so to Jim? At least, plant a seed of doubt in the old man's mind?

And why, come to think of it, was he so sure? What was giving her away? What did Walter know about Nancy that no one else knew, not even Jim or Dave? That, Kelly realized in a flash of insight, was the thing she needed to discover. But how was she going to discover it?

Maybe she was going to have to start following her *brother* around, learn more about him, understand his life, his loves, his hates, his motivations. She knew he did not in his heart want the foundry but she also knew he was unwilling to give it up to an interloper.

If she didn't find out what made Walter tick and soon, she felt certain at some deep level of her psyche, that that giant wave was going to come crashing down on her and sweep her and everything she was working so hard for out to sea.

Two weekends later, with the days gently chilling toward a windless, cloudless November and the daylight moving subtlety from crystalline to the broad flat light of winter, Kelly took out her new forest green Ford pickup for a spin. It was the first time she'd driven by herself since the accident and she felt both anticipation and trepidation. Her head bump was just a low-lying ridge on her forehead and she felt normal again, if out of shape.

Rose had driven to Denver to commiserate with an old high school friend who had just miscarried a baby and was distraught. Kelly had offered to go but Rose hadn't been in favor of it. They had discussed it the evening before over dinner.

"Jessica will feel like she isn't getting my full attention if you go, Nancy. This isn't the first time I've had to do this with her. She's been through three miserable divorces and this baby was artificially inseminated because she's decided she's gonna do it, man or no man. It's a big loss for her."

"So what are you going to do for her?"

"I'll take her out to the botanical gardens and we'll just talk for five or six hours until she can sort it through."

"You'll be home Sunday night?"

"Yes. Sunday night." Rose had given her a peck on the cheek. "Don't worry. I'll call you when I get there and when I leave, okay?"

"Okay."

So Kelly had decided to kill three birds with one stone: test her truck in the back country, get in a little hiking, and become more familiar with the New Mexico landscape she was supposed to know so well.

Despite half-drowning in Cochiti Lake, she had fallen so in love with the surrounding landscape of mesa and mountain that she was anxious to return to explore it further.

The first part of the drive—down the La Bajada escarpment on the highway and then turning off toward the lake across a broad expanse of prairie grass—brought back memories of a towel-clad Rose sitting beside her in Walter's truck. The memory was sharply poignant and she realized Rose's absence—temporary as it was—had left her feeling bereft.

It was silly, she knew, that she felt bereft at all. It was a big blinking danger sign that she was giving her heart to Rose. Hell, what did she mean 'giving'? It was a done deal. She was head over heels in love with the woman and wanted to spend every second with her.

The truck raced smoothly across the long open plain beneath the empty sky and Kelly felt inordinately proud to have such a powerful, shiny truck. It made her feel tall and special and she could not believe the strange twist of circumstances that had placed her where she was.

Despite not feeling completely well in the last two weeks—she had indeed contracted and suffered through a bad cold—she had pushed herself to finish the White account and that of the broken sword. Since then, she had started on two new accounts Jim had given her. Soon, she knew, he would be sending her out into the art community, with his blessing, to drum up her own accounts and bring in that precious new business that the foundry so desperately needed.

She took the turnoff to the dam, all the while admiring the rising blue-green lumps of the Jemez mountains to one side and the massive black lava escarpment of La Bajada to the other. Shortly, she was on the dam itself and she could see the wavy blue-green of the water far below the narrow two-lane roadway.

Walter had been right: estimating by eye where the catamaran had capsized in the lake, it would have required miles of swimming to reach either the dam or the boat ramp.

Kelly reached the far side of the dam and decided to take the access road to the overlook. There, she got out and stretched and stared down at the lake. From this angle, it was an even darker green. She strapped on her small waist pack and water bottle and headed down the marked-and-numbered nature trail which wandered among the pinon pine trees.

Down on the water, looking like multi-colored toys from the distance, was every kind of small watercraft one could imagine—sailboats, catamarans, pontoon houseboats, rowboats, canoes and even paddle boats. The handful of speedboats drifted along at an equally slow pace as the others because Cochiti Lake enforced a strict wake-free policy. All in all, she counted thirteen watercraft. She didn't know if that was considered a quiet or a busy Saturday at Cochiti.

The trail was easy and short and she soon found herself at the tiny visitor center operated by the Army Corps of Engineers. She was through the exhibit in minutes and back out on the tarmac for the short hike back to her truck.

Kelly knew this couldn't be all there was to explore, so after consulting the overlook map, she decided to drive back across the dam to a different overlook which was perched on the eastern side of the lake.

The drive to the overlook proved to be a long and circuitous one roaming through miles of empty grassland and sheer quiet. Her passage was disturbed only by the flight overhead of an occasional hawk or the jittery jump of a suicidal rabbit crossing the roadway.

The soft nipple of the aptly-named Tetilla Peak—literally *tit* in Spanish—loomed over the La Bajada ridge making Kelly think fondly of Rose's breasts and her desire to lay her head between them. The terminus of the drive proved to be well worth it. The view of the surrounding mesas and mountains was more intimate and she sensed she would visit this place many times.

The scrub grasses of buffalo and blue gamma had bleached with the colder nights of fall but still lent a pleasant yellow warmth to the scene. Gigantic growths of grey-blue chamisa which had bloomed in riotous yellow just a month back were also paling into winter. Shrubby, multi-armed, bodies of cholla cactuses were interspersed with low-growing junipers and pinon pines and here and there tumbled boulders of black lava jutted their smooth shiny faces at the sky.

The overlook pavilion itself gave more of a view of the mouth of the lake than of the lake itself. The Rio Grande, deep green, wide, and silent, flowed between the lava walls of the *Caja del Rio*. Because Kelly was high on top of the mesa, she could trace the wandering green path of the river several miles back into the 'box' out of which it flowed.

Kelly walked along the ridge, the canyon below her feet sloping gently down to the river. On the other side of the canyon, the slope was topped by 30 or 40 feet of sheer lava escarpment. Side canyons broke off from the main river, probably carved into the lava by centuries of runoff.

Across the river, a boat puttered up a side canyon and Kelly noticed a dirt road which snaked across the mesa to yet another overlook. She wondered where that canyon led and why the boat had gone there and realized she was still hungry for adventure and ready to explore more territory.

After consulting an etched metal map in the pavilion which showed a line drawing of the Jemez range and a scattering of other peaks—the Cerro Picacho, St. Peter's Dome, Boundary Peak—she downed a soda and got back in to her truck.

After wandering along the main roadway and making a few false turns, she found the unmarked roadway to the third overlook. The un-graded surface of the road was washboard but eventually she found herself high on the mesa and, once again, overlooking the river. The side canyon held wide for a distance and then narrowed into a neck before branching into what appeared to be several, even more rugged, side canyons.

There were no boats navigating the canyon at that moment. But beached on the far side was a catamaran with yellow hulls and a narrow blue stripe on the sail, looking bigger than a toy but still smaller than a full-sized boat. As near as she could tell, there was no one aboard.

Kelly looked across the lake mouth at the pavilion she had explored an hour before. It was small in the distance and she recalled how much she had enjoyed the scenery from that vantage point. All in all, it was turning out to be a very pleasant, mildly adventurous day. It was just the right amount of discovery to fit her level of energy and interest. Pleased with herself, she leaned against the hood of her truck and ate the pear she had brought with her.

When she finished it, she started on a cheese sandwich, her eyes roaming the countryside, curious if there was a trail leading down into the side canyon that would not require rock climbing equipment. It would be fun to get down to the river.

She had just polished off the sandwich when a movement caught her eye. The beached catamaran had slid into the water and its solitary sailor, who at this distance was no bigger than Kelly's thumb, was adjusting ropes to reset the sails. Kelly watched with interest as the sailor got the craft underway.

A few moments later, the catamaran floated silently beneath her heading back to the Rio Grande, the sailor now plainly visible on the aft side of the boat. Kelly stood frozen with surprise.

The sailor was Walter and she mentally kicked herself for not recognizing the blue stripe of his sail. Not that it would have made much difference. Even if she had shouted at him, he could not have heard her from this distance. Still, she might have watched the boat more avidly to see what he was doing and where he had gone while the catamaran was beached.

Come to think of it, what had he been doing up the canyon and why had he gotten off the boat? To take a piss? He could do that from the boat itself if he wanted to: it was insufficient reason to go to shore. Also, the boat had been beached for a very long time.

Certainly not to seduce a girlfriend: there was no one aboard the vessel with him. Her 'brother' wasn't exactly a naturalist, geologist, or botanist either so what had interested him in that canyon? Had he been lounging beside the boat on the shore while she ate her sandwich and she just hadn't seen him? Or had he hiked into one of the other side canyons and then returned?

Somehow, she couldn't imagine Walter doing much hiking. He seemed too lazy and he had never professed an interest in it that she was aware of. Dave had said he complained bitterly in childhood whenever Jim made him carry a backpack into the wilderness even though Nancy had thoroughly enjoyed the activity.

Kelly continued to ponder as the catamaran turned the corner of the canyon and entered the larger river. She knew she was nearly invisible atop the mesa so it didn't matter how openly she peered at the catamaran. It was as if she and Walter were in different worlds: hers high and his low, and although it was natural for humans to look down, it was not natural to look up. She very much doubted Walter would look up.

Kelly suddenly remembered her pledge to learn more about Walter and realized she was burning with curiosity to discover what he had been up to. Her sandwich finished and the catamaran long gone, Kelly hiked along the mesa top, scouting in earnest for a place to climb down.

Despite her searches, she saw no egress that would not require climbing equipment. She walked to the point at which the canyon narrowed into a neck before branching into the side canyons. She thought the neck was probably a mere 50 or 60 feet across—plenty of room for small watercraft but literally impossible to traverse by a hiker. By sight, she estimated that to get to the other side by going around the side canyons would probably amount to 40, 50 or maybe even more miles of hiking.

She scoured the opposite wall of the canyon. There was nothing immediately obvious that could have interested Walter. There weren't even trees—just slope and rock, and she realized now that, if Walter's interest had been in one of the side canyons, he could not have skirted the neck of the canyon on foot because there was no walk space. He would have had to sail the catamaran into one of the side canyons and she could not tell from her viewpoint how deep the water was at the point of the neck. Perhaps it was silted in.

That meant whatever had interested Walter could not be far from where he had beached the catamaran. Kelly finally shrugged in disappointment, stood up, and started back to her truck. Maybe all he really had been doing was taking a bathroom break. She would probably never know and it almost certainly didn't matter.

When she got back to the main road, she drove along the paved access which headed into the Jemez mountains, still intent on exploring. However, twenty minutes later, when the paved road gave way to heavily-washboarded dirt, she grew tentative. When it narrowed into little more than a track and descended into a dark cold canyon, she wondered if it was wise to proceed along roads she knew nothing about and for which she had no map.

Bringing her truck to a halt and angling slowly back and forth in the middle of the roadway in order to turn, she decided that before she went deeply into the Jemez she should consult Rose. Better yet, she would simply bring her along to play tour guide and tell her about the sights. Maybe Rose knew of an intimate spot in the Jemez where they could engage in a bit of outdoor seduction. With that thought in mind, Kelly was cheerfully occupied for the remainder of the drive home.

The following morning, Kelly sat at the table in the kitchen

FIFTEEN

of the modular, reading the Sunday paper. The sound of a key slipping into the front door lock startled her.

She was wearing only a tattered muscle shirt and boxer shorts. By the time the door had swung open, she had jumped to her feet and was poised between flying to her bedroom and hoping it was Rose, coming home early.

It was Walter. "Good morning, sis."

"What are you doing here?" She slunk back down into her chair, trying to hide her state of undress, and not give away either her embarrassment or her annoyance.

Walter looked her up and down, his frankly assessing gaze disconcerting her. His eyebrows went up at the boxer shorts and although he smirked, he didn't comment. With his thumb, he gestured over his shoulder. "I just need to get something from my office."

He went across to unlock his office door. Kelly turned back

to her paper, her concentration fragmented, her heart pounding.

Ten minutes later, Walter came out of the office and pulled the door shut behind him. Kelly glanced over her shoulder and saw there was an aluminum baseball bat resting lightly against his leg.

"Planning to hit a few?" she asked.

"Not today," he answered, his mouth twisting. "Maybe another day."

"Did you find everything you were looking for?" She rustled her paper in annoyance.

"Yeah. Did you?"

"What do you mean?" Kelly folded the paper shut. "I wasn't looking for anything."

"Then why did you come here?"

Kelly tensed, all of her senses alert. "This is my home, Walter." She turned to face him. He hadn't moved from the office door but he was twisting the head of the bat in his palm. Its base dug into the carpet, flattening the pile.

Walter snorted and swung the bat up onto his shoulder. He charged toward her. Kelly leaped to her feet and Walter stopped, inches from her face. "Someday," he threatened, "you're going to tell me who you really are."

Kelly broke out in a sweat, adrenaline pumping through her body. "You know who I am, Walter! I'm Nancy!"

This was it, she thought. His last ditch attempt to force her to admit she wasn't Nancy. She had the sudden insight that if he knew she wasn't Nancy, he would have already gone to Jim. That meant he couldn't prove it. The realization emboldened her. She stood straighter and a confident smile came to her lips.

"You should drop this, Walter. It's not going to work."

Walter's eyes bulged with astonishment. Then he threw back

his head and laughed.

Kelly frowned, disconcerted again. "Why are you laughing?"

Walter stopped laughing and leaned even closer to her face, his eyes gleaming. "You think this is all about me proving you're not Nancy, don't you?"

"Well," Kelly huffed, "isn't it? Isn't that what you've been trying to do all along?"

Walter gripped the bat with both hands and stepped back. His eyes narrowed and Kelly felt a cold menace grip her. Maybe she was wrong. Maybe Walter had some other objective. She flushed with confusion.

"I don't have to prove you're not Nancy. I know where Nancy is...and you don't."

Kelly crumpled psychologically, her eyes registering her shock. She felt as if she'd been slugged in the solar plexus.

With a triumphant smirk, Walter walked to the front door. He turned and gave her a sweet-faced grin that made shivers run up her spine.

"Have a nice day, sis." He waved and closed the door behind him.

Kelly sat down, trembling. She shook her head several times, trying to deny to herself what she had heard. Had Walter said what she thought he'd said? *I don't have to prove you're not Nancy. I know where Nancy is...and you don't.*

She lifted her empty coffee mug from the table and rose from her chair. She must have misunderstood him. But the memory of him rushing her re-played itself and she felt again that leap of terror in her chest. He had threatened her. She had not imagined it.

She poured coffee from the carafe into her cup and sipped it. Why would Walter threaten her? For that matter, why would he reveal to her with such unequivocal certainty that he knew she wasn't Nancy? Why not continue with the pretense or...was he continuing with the pretense?

She believed he still hadn't relayed his suspicions to Jim. He couldn't have. Jim would have been on her in a hot second, demanding explanations. And why not? Why hadn't he told Jim?

She knew she had genuinely startled Walter aboard the catamaran with her knowledge of the loss of Nancy's jade necklace. In fact, his shock had been so palpable she thought she had finally laid his doubts to rest.

But he had not spoken with doubt this morning. He had been certain. Absolutely certain. What had changed? More importantly, what would he do next?

She knew, at some fundamental level, that she still didn't understand Walter. She didn't understand what drove him, what he cared about, whom he loved and whom he hated, why he privately harassed her and yet, at the same time, failed to blow her cover. What did he want?

Her eyes drifted to the door from which Walter had emerged. Without thinking about it too deeply, she rose from her chair. She tried the knob. It was locked but it was a simple indoor latch. She walked to the kitchen sink and pulled a butter knife from the drain board.

Next, she was swinging open the door to his office, reassuring herself she was doing the right thing, trying not to think about her actions as questionable ones, like breaking and entering. At the most, she was invading Walter's privacy. Besides, what could she possibly hope to find?

The sight that met her eyes was prosaic. The room looked like any office anywhere except for the overlay of dust. There was a scratched birch-veneer desk with a computer and its standard accessories, a desk chair, a floor lamp, an aging couch and a half-dozen cardboard boxes stacked against the wall.

It wasn't quite in disarray but it wasn't orderly either. Piles of paper littered the desktop and the couch. Kelly felt defeated even before getting started. Surely this was a waste of time on a Sunday morning.

Nor would Walter be pleased if he came back and found her in his inner sanctum, even if it was one that he rarely visited and seemed hardly to care about. She hesitated and then shrugged. She was already here, she might as well make a cursory search.

Two hours later, Kelly was sifting through the stacked yellowing ledgers and papers in one of the cardboard boxes when a torn news clipping slipped out from beneath the sheets of a curling legal pad.

It was headlined: *Teenage Girls Disappear*. Taped to the back was a header that read *Santa Fe New Mexican* and showed a date almost eight years in the past. Kelly turned it over and read the article with interest.

"It has been reported that on Tuesday last, Barbara Freda Knox and Nancy Arlene Summerhill, both seniors at Santa Fe High, did not report to their 1:30 biology lab at the school. Friends reported that the two had last been seen leaving the open campus in a Buick Skylark to go to lunch.

They were not reported missing by their families until Wednesday morning when both families realized that the girls had not stayed at one or the other's homes on Tuesday night. Investigation by local police resulted in determining the location of the Buick Skylark, which was found parked at a Pojoaque truck stop, but the girls have not been found.

Police have emphasized that there is no evidence of foul play or of a crime having been committed but anyone seeing the girls should report their whereabouts to Detective Gutierrez of the SFPD."

Kelly put down the clipping, feeling a frisson of excitement. The story didn't reveal much but it made her feel closer to Nancy and Barbara. Somehow, it made them real. They had been real people who had had real lives and then had simply up and vanished one day.

What had happened to them? Had they realized their love for each other by this time and decided they couldn't tell their families? Had they simply run away and concealed their identity?

But why? Had they been that afraid of their parents? Or had they just been wild and crazy and decided to chuck their future? They had been seniors and it had been late spring. Kelly guessed they couldn't have been more than a month or so away from their high school graduations.

Were they even now happily living somewhere? Were they split up? Had their departure been worth it to them or had they regretted it for all the intervening years? And why hadn't they called and said they were okay? Why would anyone drive their parents—even if they hated them—mad with worry for seven years?

And, if Walter knew where Nancy was, why didn't he tell Jim? Had Nancy forbidden him to tell Jim? Had she been closer to her brother than to her father? Kelly had never gotten that impression from Dave.

Kelly put down the clipping and continued her search through the box. A few minutes later, she came across a photograph of three teenagers.

Nancy and Barbara had been real indeed and now Kelly felt like she was prying into the personal lives of people she had never known and might well never know.

It was easy to see why Dave had been startled by Kelly's appearance: except for the long hair, she and Nancy were spitting images of each other, looking eerily like identical twins. Barbara Knox, on the other hand, had been taller and willowier, with a long horsey face and thick braid which laid across her shoulder.

Between the two women, his arms around their waists, stood a young Walter. He was a grinning boy with a downy mustache, still gangly from his teenage growth spurt, not yet exhibiting the shoulder bulk and widened jaw of a mature man.

It was a happy photo, all three of them smiling for the camera, leaning eagerly forward in the manner of the young, waiting to jump on life. She turned the photo over. It read, in fading blue ink: *Me, Barb and Nanc.*

Kelly slipped the clipping and the photo back where she found them and started on the last box. Here was the same stack of ledgers and some dot-matrix-printed foundry reports. She ruffled through them, despairing of finding anything else. It was only when she had emptied the box completely that she came across a second news clipping. It was from the same newspaper and was dated three weeks later. It read:

"Girls Still At Large. It was previously reported that Barbara Freda Knox and Nancy Arlene Summerhill, both seniors at Santa Fe High, failed to show for a lab class.

To date, no eyewitness reports or tips have been received that have lead to the whereabouts of the two girls. Police report that interviews with friends and families of the girls and a search of the vehicle in which the two were last seen has produced no evidence foul play is involved in their disappearance.

Police now believe the girls ran away from home for unknown reasons."

So that had been it. The case had been closed until further evidence opened it and life in Santa Fe had gone on without the participation of Barbara Knox and Nancy Summerhill.

Commencement had commenced without them and their families had been left with nothing but the hope that someday they would receive a call. Whether it was a call heralding good news or bad news, they wouldn't know until that day. If they received a call at all. And they never had.

Kelly put the news clipping back where she had found it, closed the box and got up on stiff knees, her back creaking from sitting in a hunched posture on the floor for so many hours. She stretched and eyed Walter's office, wondering briefly if somewhere in this room there was still a clue to Walter's assertion that he knew where Nancy was.

Then she had a fresh thought. Maybe he didn't really know where Nancy was and he was just trying to frighten her. Maybe he was just plain crazy. Maybe Nancy's disappearance was what had made him crazy.

She went across to the door. There was nothing of importance in Walter's office. It was just a sad, dusty room. She locked the door and forced her mind to turn away from the anti-climactic story of Nancy and Barbara.

She glanced at her watch. It was going on 3 o'clock and she expected Rose to be home by six. Kelly wanted dinner to be special, a welcoming home feast. She showered and changed into jeans and a long-sleeved flannel shirt and gathered up her keys.

Steak, she decided, once she was in the truck and on her way. T-bones and baked potatoes and one of those bagged mixed salads and something for dessert. But what?

Raspberries, she imagined, topped with whipped cream and shards of shaved chocolate. Something rich but not so rich that they couldn't eat a different kind of dessert later.

Rose was mostly through the raspberries, savoring every bite, her full red lips turning an even richer maroon from their juice when Kelly mentioned her Saturday adventure.

"You shouldn't have been out there by yourself. You're not well enough yet." Rose reprimanded, crushing raspberries between her teeth.

"I didn't do anything too athletic. I discovered a new place I want to hike, though."

"Where?"

"It's a canyon on the other side of the river."

"Why that particular canyon?"

"It narrows and splits into smaller canyons. I spotted Walter's catamaran back there and I was just curious."

"Is this somewhere you and he used to go as kids?"

"No. That's why I'm curious," Kelly lied.

"You think he's got buried treasure or something?" Rose popped the last raspberry into her mouth and heaved a sigh of contentment. "God, that was a marvelous dinner."

Kelly laughed. "Only the best."

"The dessert was perfect." Rose took a sip of her homemade cappuccino. "So, you didn't answer my question about the buried treasure."

Kelly laughed again. "I doubt it!"

"You know, he was probably just taking a piss or something. I'd say the two of you are obsessed with each other."

Kelly smiled to cover her fear of the truth. "I'm only obsessed with you, dear."

"This canyon is on the other side of the Rio, right?"

"Right. I didn't see any way to hike down into it. It's all lava escarpment."

"I've got climbing ropes but you're a newbie and lava isn't the best kind of rock to learn on."

Kelly shrugged and decided to drop the topic. Walter's presence in that canyon had almost certainly been meaningless anyway.

Rose took another sip of her coffee and murmured under her breath.

"What did you say?" Kelly asked.

"I was thinking. Maybe we could just canoe up the Rio. But you're not in shape for that either."

Hope rekindled in Kelly. "Oh, come on. I can canoe."

Rose laughed. "How many full military push-ups can you do?"

"Plenty." Kelly snorted.

"Oh, yeah? Let's see 'em."

"I am not going to prove it to you!"

"No prove it, no canoe. You've never even been in a canoe."

"Shit!" Kelly got down on the floor and started doing push-ups. After the third one, she lay on the floor panting.

"Is that all you can do, big butch woman?" Rose teased.

"No," Kelly muttered from the floor. "My stomach is full."

"True, you shouldn't do those on a full stomach. Why don't you come back up here?" Rose had thoroughly enjoyed the view she had been afforded of her lover's back and buttocks and thighs and it had made her hot.

"What do you want me to do now?" Kelly stood over her lover's chair, her legs spread wide and her fists on her hips.

"Umm," Rose murmured, reaching for the zipper of Kelly's jeans. "This is the perfect position. Come in a little closer."

A moment later, Kelly felt Rose's palm slide back between her legs and then stroke forward. She gasped from the shock.

It had been weeks since they had made love because of her injuries and illnesses and suddenly she was suffused with heat. Even her lips felt hot. She leaned down to kiss Rose's berry-darkened lips to cool her own and when they touched she practically swooned.

"Let's go to bed," she demanded, her voice a whisper made guttural by her leaping passion.

"Hmm, lover," Rose murmured in agreement, the sound deep in her throat, "I've been waiting for weeks for those words."

On the Saturday before Thanksgiving, Rose tied her canoe

SIXTEEN

to the roof of her camper and she and Nancy headed for Cochiti Lake. The day had dawned cold but clear, the light dusting of snow that had fallen the day before still visible only on the surrounding higher mountains.

When they arrived at the Tetilla Peak boat ramp, a brisk breeze was blowing so they stayed bundled up in their jackets while they unloaded the canoe. By the time they'd loaded their gear into the canoe, the wind had stopped and the sun and effort had warmed them sufficiently to enable them to strip down to their windbreakers.

Rose parked her truck to the side of the boat ramp and they both slipped on their safety vests. While the canoe was still on dry land, she showed Nancy how to handle the oar, explaining how she would stroke—straight down into the water and back with the oar—on the opposite side from which Rose was stroking.

"It's called the Minnesota Switch. After about six strokes, we'll change sides. That keeps the canoe going more or less straight."

Once the canoe was in the water, she helped Nancy settle into the bow seat and then she settled herself in the stern. Nancy had her back to her, so it was necessary to shout instructions. Due to Nancy's inexperience, their start in the water was a jerky one.

The breeze had let up and the water was calm, which would make for easier paddling. Rose knew it was easier to learn to canoe on a lake where one wasn't fighting the natural tug of the river's current but at least there weren't any rapids on this segment of the Rio Grande.

"Slower," Rose called out. "There's a rhythm to it. Don't rush or you'll get tired."

Kelly slowed her stroke.

"That's better. Okay now, let the paddle come straight back. Don't follow the curve of the gunnel. Also, if you lift the oar out of the water when it's parallel to your hip, you'll save yourself some unnecessary effort."

Kelly tried it and realized it was easier because she was letting the water do some of the work. "It's kind of Zen," she called back.

Rose laughed. "In ten minutes, you're not going to be enjoying it as much."

"Sure I will."

Rose called, "Change over!" and Kelly lifted the dripping oar out of the water, raised it over the hull, and started stroking on the other side of the craft.

"Your aft stroke is stronger," Rose commented after a few minutes. "You're pulling the canoe in that direction. Ease up on that side, especially since we need to be angling to port.

"Okay."

There was silence for awhile, the only sound the rising and falling of oars in the water and the call of the ravens who swooped over the canyon walls.

Eventually, Rose called out. "How far are we from this canyon of yours?"

Kelly pulled her attention from the water whose undulating green had held her mesmerized thus far and looked up the river. She could see that the mouth of Walter's canyon was just starting to show around a bend of rocks. It was striking how high over their heads the lava walls of the canyon appeared. It was very different from standing on the ridge top and looking down.

She lifted her oar from the water and pointed. "It's up there, on the left." The sun was actually warm now and Kelly felt a light sheen of sweat starting under her two layers of shirts, windbreaker, and safety vest.

"Are you getting too tired?" Rose called, still paddling. Kelly dipped her oar back into the glistening green water. "No, I'm okay. How are you doing?"

"I'll make it." In another ten minutes, they were at the mouth of Walter's canyon.

"How do we turn in there?" Kelly called, mystified.

"We need to go forward another 100 feet or so and then I'll do a pry stroke. That will turn us. The moment we turn, start with your parallel stroke again."

"Okay. Tell me when."

They paddled forward and then Rose called, "Now." The canoe turned easily but the flow of water against the canoe's side began to push it downriver. "Fast and hard!" Rose shouted. "Paddle!"

Kelly felt a surge of adrenaline as she dipped her oar into the water, pulled it forth again and then, when Rose shouted to change over, rapidly repeating her motions on the other side.

Her shoulders, not prepared for the increased exertion, ached. Fortunately, several strokes later they were inside the mouth of the canyon and the force of the water was greatly lessened.

"Whew!" Rose exclaimed, sweat pouring from her forehead. "We can't stop but we can slow down a little now." They paddled in silence for a few more minutes, mostly because neither of them had enough energy to speak.

"You want to beach her up there on the right, correct?" Rose called.

"Yes," Kelly replied, trying to fix in her mind's eye where she had seen the catamaran beached. Everything looked so different from this angle.

About a 1000 yards ahead of them was the spot where the canyon started to narrow and branch into more canyons. She thought they weren't that far from the area she'd seen Walter. "Probably anywhere that looks good to you is fine, Rose."

"Okay, let's pull her in where you see that sandbar and we'll take a break. If that's not close enough to where you want to be, we'll go up a little farther later."

Moments later they had splashed their way out of the canoe and pulled it ashore. Kelly was surprised at the stiffness of her legs and the burning pain in her shoulders. She swung and stretched her arms while Rose pulled cans of electrolyte-replacement soda and sandwiches from their stores.

"Let's sit on those rocks over there." Her hands laden, she gestured with her chin. Kelly was only too happy to sit and eat.

"That was a workout," she mouthed between bites of sandwich.

"You thought you were in shape, didn't you?" Rose teased.

"Shit. I'd have to do that every weekend to be in shape for it."

"A lot of people do that," Rose agreed. "We can do it more often if you like. I haven't been out in the canoe since earlier in the summer. Ever since you came to the foundry, I've been too distracted to go canoeing."

"Sure," Kelly said. "Blame it on me."

"It's a gorgeous day for November, isn't it?"

"Yeah." The few wisps of clouds in the sky were high and scattered and it was warm along the canyon wall where the sun struck directly, heating the rocks.

Kelly downed the last of her soda. "Did you bring dessert?"

"Sheesh," Rose complained, "you sure are demanding!"

"C'mon," Kelly insisted, "what'd you bring?"

"Chocolate-oat bars. You need the carbohydrates to replace the ones you burned."

"I'm already starting to feel better." Kelly cozied up to the rock she was settled against and closed her eyes.

Rose left her alone to nap for a few minutes while she went to get the energy bars from the canoe. She had also brought apples, which she sat and sliced into quarters while Kelly dozed.

When she was finished preparing them, she sat back and relaxed, staring out over the rich green of the river, relishing its quiet lapping against the narrow width of sand at her feet. She sighed deeply. This was why she went out into nature: to enjoy a vast quiet, empty of human sounds, but replete with nature's: water lapping, trees rustling, birds swooping, sand shifting, small mammals breathing and moving about their daily lives.

She too soon fell asleep, the bars and apples on her lap.

"Hey." There was a tender whisper at her ear and Rose came back to wakefulness.

"You were out," Kelly said to her startled face.

Rose sat up. "It's so lovely here. I feel like I'm drinking in the sky and the water and the rocks."

"You are, lover." Kelly had slipped behind her and was cradling her hips against hers, her arms circling Rose's belly. "I'd like to drink you in, too, but I don't think there's anywhere flat enough to really do it properly."

"Umm," Rose murmured. "Let's do it as soon as we get home."

"In that case," Kelly said, "we'd better have our dessert and then get hopping." She reached for a quarter of apple and the two of them munched the food in silence, enjoying the beauty of the desert surroundings.

When they were done, Rose put the remains of their lunch in the canoe and joined Kelly where she stood on the edge of the steep hillside.

"Are we close enough to where you saw Walter?"

"I think if we walk up just a ways, we'll be at the spot where he beached the cat."

There was no trail and they found themselves clambering over rocks and around cactuses, Kelly alert for the location she thought Walter had landed his boat.

"Look," she finally shouted. "There's a little sandbar there. That's probably it."

They walked down the steep hill of scrub grass until they'd reached the sandbar. Here, the hillside curved away into one of the side canyons, blocking their view.

"Do you think he hiked into the side canyon?"

"I guess so. But there aren't any tracks here or anything so it's hard to tell."

"The water would have washed them away."

"Probably. Do you see a trail?"

"No."

"Maybe he was just clambering around the rocks, like we are."

Kelly's eyes scanned upward, toward the ledge of rock that formed the top of the canyon. "He couldn't have climbed out onto the mesa without climbing equipment. The only way into these canyons is by water."

"You know," Rose said, also looking up, "if we can go over or behind that huge boulder, maybe we will find a way into the side canyon, below the escarpment. If not, we can just turn back and call it a day."

"Okay. Sounds like a plan to me."

They climbed the steep hillside again. When they reached the boulder, Rose took the lead. "Usually the surface of this kind of rock is bumpy enough that you can find handholds." She pointed. "I think if we go this way, we'll be able to scale it pretty easily. Are you up for it?"

"Sure," Kelly smiled. "It doesn't look that hard."

"That's what everybody says until they're in the middle of a rock and they can't figure out how to go up or down."

"Sounds scary."

"Yeah. That's the moment when you find out what you're really made of."

"So, I take it that means you know what you're really made of."

"Of course I do! I just don't know what you're made of."

"Well, if you're going to be that way about it, get out of my way, girlfriend and I'll show you what I'm made of."

Rose giggled. "You butches are all the same: lots of talk and no action."

Kelly grabbed Rose around the middle and pulled her into a hard embrace. "You're going to have to take that remark back," she ordered when she came up for air.

Rose was breathless. "No."

"Damn," Kelly kissed her hard again, this time locking her

head into place with her hands. When she released her, she demanded, "How about now?"

"Umm, okay." Rose had a teasing glint in her eye. "I didn't know you were into the rough stuff."

"I'm very versatile. I can do anything you want."

"Hmm," Rose returned, "With that in mind, I'm going to have to start planning for what I want."

Kelly lifted an eyebrow. "Do you want to do it right here?"

"No. I want to climb this rock, go home, and take full advantage of the softness of my bed for the activities I have in mind."

Kelly laughed. "Okay. Let's climb this damn rock."

With Rose leading the way, they scaled the boulder and found themselves on the other side which opened to a vista that had previously been invisible. The canyon snaked back, the walls tight on each side, the lava escarpment giving a 20 to 30 foot high black trim to the mesa top.

It was cooler in the side canyon because more of the sun was blocked by the western wall of the canyon. The escarpment, though, was in full sunlight. Looking up, Kelly saw a dark vertical demarcation in the escarpment.

"Maybe you can climb to the top of the mesa through that gap," she said, pointing.

"Sure, let's try it. There's no evidence Walter ever came back here, Nancy. I mean there doesn't seem to be a trail or anything. He was probably just taking a piss, you know, and you couldn't see him."

"Yeah, probably. I'd actually completely forgotten about him. I never really expected to find anything out here. I mean, what could we find anyway?"

A few minutes later, they had reached the gap in the escarpment and, much to their surprise, they discovered it was not a gap in the lava that would permit a chimney climb to the mesa top. Instead, it was an opening that widened into a cave.

It was much cooler in the cave than outside, and the light that filtered in from the entrance was dim but they could immediately tell that the cave contained evidence of human—modern, not ancient—occupation. There was an open cardboard box of supplies that included a Sterno stove, matches, candles, rope, canned foods, and oddly, plastic flowers.

"What are these for?" Kelly lifted them out of the box.

"That's nothing. Look at this." Rose had drifted toward the back of the unevenly-shaped space and was looking down at a crude white cross that had been dug partially into the hard packed dirt floor.

"What is it?" Kelly dropped the flowers back into the box and joined Rose at the back of the cave.

"It looks like a grave marker."

"A grave marker? That's pretty bizarre."

"B.K.," Rose read. "I wonder what B.K. stands for? Do you think someone named B.K. is buried here or do you think it's just someone's strange way of remembering him or her?"

"Her...oh, my god." Kelly felt her stomach heave and she was hit by a wave of intense claustrophobia, as though the roof and walls of the cave were closing in on her.

"Let's get the hell out of here!"

"Jeez, Nancy—"

"Yeah, *Nancy*, what's the hurry?"

Nancy turned toward the entrance of the cave, her mind filling with horror.

The entrance to the cave was blocked by a figure back-lit by

SEVENTEEN

the sun. Rose could not immediately decipher who it was, but Kelly was in a different mental world, a world of utter clarity. Even so, she could not comprehend Walter's sudden immense and menacing size. It had to be either a trick of the light and the small size of the cave or her overwhelming paranoia.

Today was not the day Kelly wanted to die, but she knew instinctively that that was what Walter had in store for her, just as he had had for Barbara Knox, whose grave they had stumbled across. The aluminum baseball bat resting against his leg told her everything she needed to know.

"I'm so glad you got yourselves here," Walter remarked, twisting the bat in his hand so that it scraped a circle in the dirt, just as it had done in Kelly's carpet. "It makes this so much easier."

Rose stepped forward. "What are you doing here, Walter? Are you following us?"

"I think you should ask your *girlfriend* those questions."

Rose turned to look at Nancy, whom she could see—even in the poor light—had turned a bilious shade of green and stood bent over, clutching her stomach.

"Nancy!" Rose was alarmed. "Are you okay? What happened?" She ran to Nancy's side.

"Her name isn't really Nancy, Rose. She's been fooling you."

Rose backed away from Nancy. "Okay. This is too weird." "What in the hell is going on here?"

Walter grinned, his eyes shiny. "Why don't you tell her, whatever-your-name-is?"

Rose moved closer to the silent Nancy again and pleaded in a low voice. "Honey, what's going on?"

Still clutching her stomach, Kelly lowered herself to the dirt, sitting on her knees. "I meant to tell you, Rose. Somehow. I just didn't know how."

Rose knelt beside her. "Tell me what?"

"Walter's right. I'm not Nancy."

Rose's head reeled with incomprehension. "What do you mean? How could you not be Nancy? Mr. Summerhill—"

Walter gave a hoot of laughter. "That old man wouldn't care if she had six heads as long as she claimed she was Nancy and could turn the foundry back from economic ruin!"

"Which you sure as hell weren't doing!" Rose stood up and rushed toward Walter. Walter, ever so infinitesimally, raised the bat. Rose stopped dead.

"Christ, Walter! What do you think you're doing? Are you going to keep us in here with that...that bat? How scared of you do you think we are?"

"Rose," Kelly almost whispered, "we should be real scared of Walter. Don't antagonize him."

"I don't believe this!" Rose screeched. "He's your brother!

What is he going to do? Hit us?"

Walter laughed again, a high hee-hawing kind of laugh.

"Rose, Walter is not my brother and I am not Nancy. That grave marker you saw with the letters, B.K.—" Kelly's eyes were closely watching Walter, "the B.K. stands for Barbara Knox. Doesn't it, Walter?"

Walter didn't say anything, but his grin widened.

"Barbara Knox! I thought she left you high and dry in South Dakota!"

"Rose," Kelly was shouting now, "for the last time, I'm not Nancy!"

The information had finally penetrated and Rose felt cold suffuse her body and raise goose bumps on her arms. The change wasn't from the temperature in the cave. It was from the deep primal fear that was growing inside her.

"Well, if you're not Nancy, who are you? And where's Nancy?" Her voice was low and breathless.

Kelly looked at Walter, his voice still echoing in her brain from that morning when he had threatened her: *I know where Nancy is...and you don't.* "Where is Nancy, Walter?"

Walter twirled the bat against the ground and looked down at the patterns he was making in the dirt. "Nancy is at the bottom of Cochiti Lake."

There was a complete and total silence. Kelly dropped her head, mourning—not for the first but the third time—for this woman she had never met. Rose stood with her mouth open.

"Why did you kill her?" Kelly asked softly.

"She stole my girlfriend."

The answer was so simple, so succinct, and so chilling, Kelly could not at first process it. Rose was still mystified.

"Who was your girlfriend?"

"Barbara Knox."

"You killed her too, didn't you?" It was Kelly again, her voice low and shocked, but certain.

"She was going to report me."

"They went sailing with you that day, didn't they? They ditched school and you picked them up in Pojoaque and you all went sailing."

Walter went along with her in a kind of dream state, remembering, as if he were seeing that day again, a day he must have repeated a million times in his imagination.

"Yes, it was sheer accident that I saw them there. I was working a dig by myself for my archeology class up by Abiquiu and I was driving back to school. They were just getting into my Skylark to go back to class after eating lunch. It wasn't planned or anything. It was just such a beautiful day and I said, 'School, schmool. My cat's at the lake, let's go sailing.'"

His eyes were distant. "They hopped into my Jeep and I made them lay down so they wouldn't be seen while we drove through town."

"So you were already planning to kill them."

Walter frowned. "I wasn't planning to kill them. I didn't want a truant officer to see the three of us and stop us for ditching. Why would I want to kill them?"

Kelly mentally kicked herself for breaking Walter's storytelling mood. Now he probably wouldn't go on to explain why what had happened had happened. Still, somehow she already knew: it must have been at the lake that his sister had innocently revealed her infatuation with Barbara Knox.

That's when the trouble must have started. Still, she would prefer him to confirm it. "I'm sorry, Walter," she apologized in the most contrite voice she could muster, "Go on."

"We went out on the lake—" Walter's whole demeanor changed, the dreamy recollection halted, and Kelly knew he wasn't going to say anymore.

"Well, something went wrong," Rose blurted, trying to make sense of what she was hearing. Walter shifted his weight and looked at her with menace.

"I'm going to give you a choice, Rose."

"What are you talking about?"

"You can marry me and never discuss with anyone what I'm about to do or I'll have to do the same thing to you. Which is it going to be?"

Rose turned to Kelly, her face creased with confusion. "What is he going to do?"

"He's going to kill me, Rose. If you don't marry him, he's going to kill you, too."

"What! But why?"

"Because," Kelly figured there was no reason not to put her finger on Walter's deep-seated psychopathic problem, "I stole his girlfriend."

Walter nodded, satisfaction at her understanding of him and the insanity that drove him, almost showing on his face.

"Who is his girlfriend?" Rose was still incomprehending.

"Rose, you are his girlfriend," Kelly patiently explained.

Rose turned to Walter to plead. "Walter, it was a ruse! You know that! It was to fool Jim Summerhill."

"No, Rose, it wasn't. I'm in love with you. I want you to marry me."

"But you're going to kill Nancy!"

"She's not Nancy. Don't worry about her. Look. Just wait outside. I'll be done in a minute. Never breathe a word of it and everything will be fine. We'll be happy, I promise." He lifted the bat. "Just get out of the cave."

"Are you out of your mind?" Something quite clearly had snapped in Rose and she rushed Walter. But he was already poised to take a lethal swing at her.

"Shit!" Kelly leaped to her feet and threw herself at Walter's shins with the hope of throwing him off his balance and knocking him backward from the cave mouth. She succeeded but not before she heard the bat connect with some part of Rose's body.

She didn't have time to look back because she was skidding down the slope after Walter, who was traveling on his back, the bat still firmly in his hand. He was trying to stop and right himself, screaming obscenities at her, but he couldn't seem to slow the pull of gravity.

Nor could she. Grass and rocks flew by and her right arm tore across the top of a cactus, which although it sliced through her clothes to her flesh, failed to stop her violent tumbling descent.

Walter hit the water only seconds before she did and as she went under she felt the cold as a shock that ripped the breath from her lungs, just as she had that day aboard the catamaran, except that the water was even colder now.

She came up for air only to find herself less than 10 feet from Walter whose face was contorted with rage. "You're going to die, bitch!" he shouted.

She turned and swung out her trembling arms to swim for the shore which seemed so close. The hollow weightless bat was floating in the water only two arm lengths ahead of her. If only she could reach it in time...

But Walter's hand was on her shoulder, clawing at her clothes, pulling her back toward him. "Walter," she screamed, "we'll both drown!"

His laugh was maniacal. "I'm not going to drown, bitch, but you are." He turned her in his arms—which were far stronger than her ability to fight him off—and she could see that he was bleeding from his nose and from a wound above his eye, where he had probably caught a rock or a cactus.

"Walter," she tried again, her mouth going down toward the water as he pushed, "think!"

He laughed, his eyes bright with his insanity, and pushed her under. Adrenaline pounded through her body as her open mouth filled with water. She grabbed for his torso and dug her nails deep into his sides. Walter shot out of the water and she too bobbed upward, desperately flailing her arms in an attempt to put as much distance between them as possible.

She had just cleared the surface of the water and hauled in a deep water-choked breath, when he came at her again. This time, a look of violent hatred on his features, he simply brought his fist forward and slugged her full in the face. She reeled back in the water, her head spinning, feeling the blood burst from her nose, knowing, with a sudden certainty, that she was going to die.

She couldn't fight him. He only had to push her under one more time and keep her there. Which is exactly what he did. As her mind closed down into darkness, she fought anyway, kicking and hitting her assailant.

What Kelly never saw was Rose rushing down the hillside, Rose picking up the bat, which had drifted to shore and Rose bringing the bat down hard on Walter's head. Rose both heard and felt Walter's skull crack from a blow that she had delivered out of vast reserves of adrenaline and rage.

Walter's head and startled features disappeared beneath the surface and blood flowed everywhere, tinging the water. Rose knew Walter must have lost hold of Nancy but she didn't see her come up to the surface.

Driven by terror, Rose dived into the murky green water and, after what seemed forever, found Kelly sinking toward the colder bottom waters, already moving along with the current toward the larger river.

Rose had taken water safety in high school and knew how to do a water carry and CPR. In moments that seemed like hours, she got Kelly onto the sandbar and started pumping water from her lungs. Miraculously, Kelly's heart was still beating and Rose prayed it had not been too long that she had been deprived of oxygen.

Finally, after several minutes of pumping, she saw Kelly's chest lift with her own breath and tears burst from Rose's eyes. "Oh, goddess, she's going to live. I don't care," she swore to all of the universe that was listening, "if she's brain-dead. I will always live with her and take care of her. For all of her life and all of my life. I don't care if she's Nancy. I don't care who she is. I love her."

Kelly gurgled and rolled onto her side, coughing and hacking.

Rose knelt beside her. "I'm going to pull you into the water and water-carry you to the catamaran which must be around the corner and then we'll get out of here. You don't have to do anything but let me carry you. Can you do that?"

Kelly nodded, not able to speak.

Rose didn't know how to sail the catamaran but after she'd half-dragged, half-shoved Kelly aboard it, she pulled it into the water and loosened the jib in the hopes that the wind would figure out which way to push them and that the flow of the river would take them back to the lake. Kelly lay on the deck, shivering as she had the previous time, and Rose prayed that they would find help soon.

It was only then that she realized that she was struggling to breathe and she made the guess that the radiating pain in her shoulder and right side meant Walter had broken something—maybe a rib—with the bat.

After being knocked on the ground by the force of his blow, she had felt no pain and not thought of it again. She had felt no pain because she didn't have time to feel it.

At first, it was the current that took them out to the river but once they were in the lake, they started drifting toward the dam. Rose, not knowing enough about setting the sails, could not make the catamaran turn toward shore.

Finally, her voice hoarse from shouting, she had the good fortune to attract the attention of a sailboarder.

When the man realized the two women were in the middle of an emergency, he tied his sailboard to the catamaran, boarded her, and set the sails to take them back to the boat dock.

Miraculously, or so Rose thought, he had a cell phone stashed deep in a waterproof lining, strung with other gear over his shoulder. He called 911 and by the time they reached the main boat dock, an ambulance was waiting to provide emergency treatment and take them to the hospital.

It was only once they were safely stowed in the ambulance and racing toward Albuquerque with sirens blaring, that Rose even remembered about Walter and what she had done to him.

How could she ever explain what had happened? She didn't believe it herself.

Five days later, the Summerhill family did not gather for

EIGHTEEN

Thanksgiving. Instead, Dave Paxton led a brief memorial service for Walter Summerhill at the boat ramp of Cochiti Lake which was attended by Jim Summerhill, his wife Alice, and a handful of Walter's friends.

Kelly Bransford, who remained in the hospital recovering from bacterial pneumonia and Rose Twill, who had sustained a broken collarbone and three broken ribs, and who was staying by Kelly's bedside, did not attend.

Walter's body had been recovered and cremated and Dave, on behalf of Jim, had scattered the young man's ashes over the water that he had loved so much.

Jim Summerhill had been informed by authorities that the odds of locating Nancy Summerhill's remains after so many years, which could now be believed to repose somewhere in the lake, were not equal to the time and expense that would be involved in doing so.

It had taken Jim every hour of the previous four days to accommodate himself to the reality that he should leave Nancy's body to its rest in the lake. But he had told Dave that in the spring, when he was more able bear the pain of his losses, he would make plans for a bronze memorial for Nancy.

The skeletal remains of Barbara Knox had been disinterred earlier in the week and, after the completion of volumes of paperwork on the part of the Office of the Medical Investigator, had been turned over to the Knox family to make whatever arrangements they desired for her formal internment.

Jim Summerhill's eyes were empty of tears as he stared across the placid green waters that had claimed both of the children of his body. He had not had time to adjust to the fact that his son, now dead himself, had murdered his daughter.

He had long ago accepted that the odds were, in a violent and unpredictable world, that the missing teenaged Nancy had met her end by foul play. Still, he hadn't formally mourned for her in a ceremony. But today, with renewed pain, he was mourning for the loss of Nancy with certainty, not speculation. Mourning for her lost adulthood and, in a confused unclear way, for the brother who had murdered her.

Looking back, he could not believe how welcoming a living 'Nancy' back into his life could have ended in a tragedy of this magnitude. He realized now that he had believed Kelly Bransford to be Nancy because it had been the most profound wish of his heart that she be his daughter, restored to him after all these years. On that glorious day that that young woman had walked into his office, he had felt like an invigorated man.

A man who had something to believe in again, something to live for, something to be and share. And 'Nancy' had met his every expectation. She had loved the art that he loved and had devoted his life too. But she wasn't Nancy, she wasn't his daughter...it was another loss, another child to mourn, even if it wasn't his child.

Though not religious by inclination, on that day of her appearance he had felt like the father in the parable of the Prodigal Son, rejoicing that his lost progeny had returned to the fold.

Yet all of the time, there had been a wolf in the fold and that wolf had been his own son. His son had always known what had happened to the real Nancy. Walter had not only always known what had become of Nancy, he had perpetrated the deed himself. Jim Summerhill did not know how he could have loved and reared so monstrous a son.

Jim Summerhill looked across the inoffensive waters and felt old and disconsolate and didn't know why he wasn't dead instead of his children. At that moment, it would have been far preferable to him. He wanted to scream at the mesas and hills and waters that life had cheated him, had cheated him of his children.

The only thing he was thankful for on this Thanksgiving Day was that his first wife, the mother of Walter and Nancy, wasn't alive to meet this horrible day and to know what their son had done.

Unlike a person of able body—and Jim Summerhill deeply and bitterly regretted this—he could not go home today and kill himself.

Two days before Christmas, Rose Twill—who had originally been arraigned on a charge of second-degree murder and released on the bond that Dave had put up— was notified that the District Attorney's office had determined that the deathof Walter

Summerhill constituted justifiable homicide under the law.

Kelly Bransford, who had originally been charged with criminal intent to defraud as a result of her impersonation scheme, was notified that the District Attorney did not intend to pursue a criminal charge but that she should be aware that she might be liable for civil damages should Jim Summerhill or the Summerhill Foundry choose to pursue the matter.

Kelly had been released from the hospital eleven days after her near-drowning and Dave had taken both her and Rose in, putting them up in his Albuquerque apartment. The media had had a field day with their story and neither of them could face returning to Santa Fe, not that they expected they would be exactly welcomed at the foundry.

The moment she was able to move around without the breathlessness and pain caused by her injuries, Rose found work cashiering at a gas station, taking a full day shift and a graveyard shift. She had sat at Kelly's side in the hospital but once Kelly was out of danger, she found she couldn't face her former lover. She came home to Dave's apartment at odd hours only to sleep.

Kelly puttered away at her potter's wheel in Dave's backyard, too deep in grief over the loss of Rose and her own deception of Jim to speak. She lost weight steadily and coughed frequently, not caring if she lived or died. She had abandoned her few worldly goods at the foundry and fully expected the truck Jim had bought her to have been repossessed.

Christmas came and went without presenting so much as a blip on the radar screens of any of the three, including Dave, who had not ceased wrestling with his conscience since that horrible Saturday in November when he'd been called as 'next of kin' to University Hospital in Albuquerque at the request of Kelly.

Everything that had happened was his fault and he cursed the day that he had seen Kelly Bransford standing on the Plaza, selling her pottery. He cursed his desire to make Jim happy, knowing now that it had been a flawed desire from the start. All that he had accomplished was the death of Walter and the sure closing of the foundry. It was only a matter of time before Jim made up his mind to sell it and get out because he had no one to run it and because it held too many unbearable memories.

On February 5th of the new year, Dave, Kelly and Rose each received an invitation from Alice to attend a Valentine's Day party at the foundry. The invitation made it clear that they were not so much invited as being required to attend. The night they received the invitation was the first night they all sat together around Dave's kitchen table—even though it was 10:30 p.m.—and spoke to each other.

"I'll have to take the damn day off," Rose complained, not looking at either of them, but glaring at the invitation. Crow's feet were starting to form around her eyes and her skin was grey with exhaustion.

"He's going to crucify me," Dave said, "and I deserve it."

"It doesn't matter," Kelly pointed out, her head on the table, "what he says or what he's going to do. Let's just get it over with. Our lives are already in the toilet. Nothing could make it any worse."

They went together, mostly for support, but spoke little on the 60 mile drive. At one point, Dave flipped on the radio to oldies music and then three minutes later, switched it off again.

As they got closer to Santa Fe, they could see there were dirty crusts of leftover snow lining the roadway. By the time they arrived at the foundry, the sun was sinking into the winter quiescence of early afternoon and the air had grown cold. Once at the foundry, Kelly noticed, much to her surprise, that her new truck was still parked in the driveway of the modular.

Alice greeted them at the front door of the house—which was seldom used except for company—and promptly offered them some of the alcohol-laced ginger ale punch that sat on the table in a crystal bowl. The living room had been decorated in the traditional holiday colors of red and pink and white and floated with crepe paper and cutout hearts.

A fire roared in the fireplace and the atmosphere was cozy. They took seats on the couch while Alice made small talk, asking them innocuous questions about their work and their activities in Albuquerque.

When they had finished their first round of drinks, Alice refilled their glasses and offered them plates of crackers with cheese and smoked salmon on toast. They were all beginning to feel more relaxed from the effects of the alcohol but none of them dared ask after Jim.

Eventually, as though responding to an inner call, Alice excused herself and ten minutes later, while her guests sat in an inebriated anxious silence, she wheeled Jim Summerhill into the room.

Rose felt sheer terror at the sight of the old man and hurriedly set her drink on the coffee table so she wouldn't drop it; Kelly's stomach stirred with nausea; and Dave's spine stiffened.

"So," Jim started, an out-of-context grin on his face, "Alice pestered you enough that you were finally able to be bothered to come and visit the lonely old quadriplegic who gave you all jobs."

Dave's heart plummeted into his stomach. "Jim, you know we—"

"Shush up, Dave," the old man's eyes grew cold. "We'll get to you later. First, I'm talking to Rose." Rose wrung her hands and stared down at the table. "Young lady, you killed my son."

Rose gurgled and her face blanched.

"This has been hard for me to come to and it has taken some time, but I agree with the DA that his death seemed to have been in the best interest of Kelly's—and your own—survival. Now," he went on, his face harsh, "you owe me something. I want to know why all of this happened. I don't want the media's endless speculations about the facts. I want the truth."

"Oh, god," Rose murmured under her breath, her face now in her hands.

Kelly's heart was pounding and she stole a glance at Rose.

"Mr. Summerhill," Kelly intervened. "Do you really want to know the truth?"

Jim turned his eyes on Kelly. "Yes, I do. We can, none of us, go on without the truth."

"It won't be pleasant," Kelly said, her mouth dry.

"Nothing about this matter has been pleasant, Kelly."

"Mr. Summerhill," Rose had found her voice again even though she felt as though she was throwing herself from a high cliff, "I was dating Walter as a cover. I'm...I'm a lesbian. Everything went fine until Nancy came to the foundry—" she glanced at Kelly "—and then...well, I fell in love with her."

Jim Summerhill's eyes snapped briefly with distaste but he didn't seem surprised by the revelation. "Go on."

"In the cave that day, Walter told me that if I agreed to marry him and never told anyone about his murdering Kelly—and by implication the other women—then everything would be all right."

"Did he know you were in love with Kelly?"

"He—"

"—he suspected it for a long time," Kelly interrupted, "because he began making threats to me—sometimes to both of us—

far earlier."

"I'm not an investigator, Kelly," Dave put in. "But I checked over your truck at the junkyard after it was totaled. The tie rod cotter key pins were missing and there was a series of pin-sized holes in the brake fluid line. I didn't know if any of that meant anything but I did report it to the police. I don't know if they ever investigated."

"Maybe," Alice offered, "it made them more apt to believe that Rose and Kelly had been threatened by Walter and acted in self-defense."

"Maybe," Jim agreed, "but it was more likely they accepted the argument of self-defense because Kelly's nose had been broken and she nearly drowned."

A cold shiver raced up Kelly's spine. Her nose had healed but it was still swollen and showed a hard jag at the bridge that she knew would be with her for the rest of her life.

Jim went on. "Was Walter in love with you, Rose?"

"He said he was but he knew I was a lesbian from the start."

"From the start?"

"I met Walter in a gay club in Santa Fe—"

"Christ!" Jim sputtered. "Was my son gay too?"

Rose shook her head. "I don't think so. I think he just liked to pick up gay women. I don't know why—maybe it was more of a challenge or safer or something. In any case, he offered me a job in the foundry, but told me I'd have to date him while I worked here because—" Rose looked embarrassed.

"—because?" Jim's eyes probed her for the answer.

"—because you were supposedly so homophobic that you would fire me if you found out."

Jim snorted in disbelief. "Homophobic? Why didn't I fire Dave? The guy couldn't be more queer! In fact, I took him in because he was queer. How homophobic is that?"

"I didn't know about Dave until—" Rose glanced at Kelly.

"Jim," Dave reasoned, "you've always believed that a woman needs a man—"

"And I still do. That doesn't mean I fire a good employee because of it!"

Kelly spoke up. "I heard the homophobia story too, Mr. Summerhill. Dave himself told me."

Jim was so annoyed, his eyes seemed to blaze. "I don't care what any of you do as consenting adults! I can't believe you wouldn't know that, Dave."

"Mr. Summerhill," Kelly interjected gently, "It was Walter who was the real homophobe, even if he did pick up gay women. He killed his sister because in his mind she had stolen his girlfriend, Barbara. When he saw the same thing happening again with Rose, the thought of killing the competitor for her affections just repeated itself for him. I don't think he saw any other solution."

"That's mental illness," Alice said quietly.

"Yes," Kelly agreed, "I believe Walter didn't know what he was doing. He was pathologically jealous over both Barbara and Rose and he saw Nancy and myself as competitors. Maybe he felt he could control female competitors but not male ones. Either that or it was just quirky that he had the misfortune to fall in love with lesbians."

"All right," Jim said. "At least now I understand what happened. And, Rose, I may not be crazy about your relationship with Kelly, but it doesn't mean you can't work for me."

"But," Rose spoke before she thought, "I'm not working for you."

"You're damn rights you're not and I need that rectified immediately. This business is going down the tubes, Rose!"

Rose had risen from the couch, a look of complete

dumbfoundedness on her face. "You'll take me back?"

Jim's mouth was set belligerently. "What did I just say?"

Rose subsided and settled back down on the couch, "Yes, sir. Can I start next week?"

"Next week will be fine." The old man didn't miss a beat. "Now, Dave Paxton, as for you, you owe me an explanation. I took you in as a young man and yet you connived with Kelly Bransford here to steal the foundry from its rightful heir, namely Walter Summerhill."

Dave hung his head. "I have no defense."

"Damn you, Dave! Your defense had better be that you thought this Nancy look-alike could restore the foundry."

"I only had one thought, Jim. I thought she would make you happy."

At that, Jim started to laugh. It was a brazen, big-bellied laugh and all of them were startled, even Rose who looked lighter and brighter than she had in months. Just looking at her, Kelly felt a stirring in her heart. Just as quickly, it turned to ashes. Jim needed Rose, but he didn't need her.

In another minute, he would be sending her packing. She had known all along that this moment would come: no one would tolerate someone who had bald-facedly deceived them.

That's was why she couldn't fathom why her new truck was still in the yard. She couldn't imagine Jim letting her take the truck. Maybe he'd decided to purchase it for himself.

"Jim," Dave implored, "why is that so funny? I totally fucked this up and you know it."

"Yeah," Jim had calmed down, "I was real darned pissed at you, David Paxton. There you went sticking this gift horse right under my nose knowing full well I was going to be too damn ecstatic over it to ever look it in the mouth. But that," he went on, sobering, "was my fault as much as yours."

"What do you mean?"

"It means, Dave, that we're getting to be such old codgers that it didn't occur to us to look any deeper into Kelly here. You, at least, thought of it before I did."

Dave shook his head, mystified. "I'm still not following you."

"Dave, what did Kelly say to you that made you send away for archived records from the *Trinidad Record*?"

"The *Trinidad Record*? Holy shit, I'd forgotten I wrote to them."

"Well, they didn't forget. About six weeks ago, they sent the print of the microfiches you'd requested."

"Six weeks ago?"

Alice spoke up. "Dave, you weren't here and the envelope was addressed to the foundry so I opened it. It didn't mean anything to me so I showed it to Jim."

Dave's eyes were glinting with sudden comprehension. "Well?" he demanded.

Kelly was watching them in befuddlement, wondering what this odd sidetrack had to do with her imminent banishment.

Jim, unable to contain himself, grinned. "Paydirt, Dave!" he crowed. "You hit paydirt!"

Dave jumped to his feet. "You're kidding me!"

"No," Jim's eyes were shining. "No, I'm not. The newspaper archives didn't tell me anything I didn't already know, of course, and I puzzled over them for days—wondering what you could possibly want with them—until I made the connection. When I did, I hired a private investigator. His report came back about two weeks ago and his findings are conclusive. She is exactly who you think she is, Dave."

"What are we talking about?" Kelly asked, her forehead wrinkled in a deep frown.

"Oh, holy shit, Kelly! This is incredible news." Dave reached down to pull Kelly to her feet and she found herself standing with Dave's hands on her shoulders and his bright eyes staring into hers.

"What's incredible news?" Rose stood up too, her face a mask of consternation.

"Dave," Kelly repeated, "what's going on?"

"You're a Summerhill, kiddo." Dave almost whispered the phrase, as though it were a sacred one.

"What?"

"Kelly," Jim explained, "you're the biological daughter of my sister Arlene. Arlene was killed in an accident in Trinidad, Colorado apparently just a few months after you were born."

"But I was adopted at birth." Kelly still looked mystified.

"Yes, you were. Arlene was estranged from our parents and was on her own. I was away, on active duty in the army. None of us knew she had gotten pregnant—she never told anyone—or that she hadgiven her baby up for adoption. Maybe she planned to tell someone someday, but she was killed before anyone in the family ever learned of it."

Rose stared at Jim, unable to absorb all of the information. "Who did you say this person Arlene was?"

"Arlene," Jim repeated slowly, "was my baby sister. Kelly is her daughter. In other words, Kelly is my niece."

"Holy shit," Kelly breathed. She was suddenly dizzy and had to sit down.

"Well," Rose started to laugh hysterically, "I guess something had to explain the uncanny resemblance to Nancy." She put her hand to her forehead and stared at Kelly. "This is like a twisted game show. First I find out you're not person number one and now I find out you aren't entirely person number two, whom I didn't even get a chance to know. Now, I find out you're person number three, someone you don't even know. Who the hell are you, anyway?"

Kelly was deeply shaken. "I don't know. I know my name is Kelly Bransford, I know I'm not Nancy Summerhill, but apparently I'm...well, I guess I'm Nancy's first cousin."

"It's our fault really," Jim said. "The resemblance alone should have caused Dave and me to investigate Kelly's origins earlier. Of course, I didn't have as much knowledge as Dave. I didn't know Kelly wasn't Nancy and I didn't know that she was adopted. I only learned all of that after Walter's death."

"Yes," Dave said, "on that black day when I had to tell you the truth."

"People," Jim lectured, "things have been hard, very hard. But we can't live in the past any more. It's over and gone. We have to make the choice to go forward into the future. So, my question to you, Ms. Kelly Bransford, is: are you willing to inherit the foundry, after all? You are a Summerhill and I have no heir."

"Inherit the foundry? My god, Mr. Summerhill, I'd be happy just to be allowed to work here."

Jim laughed. "All right then, Kelly. On one condition."

"One condition. What's that?" She knew the crunch was coming. Despite his earlier protestations, he would forbid her and Rose to live together while they worked for him.

"You have to start calling me Jim. Dad is too painful and 'Mr. Summerhill' is too formal. You can put Uncle in front of the Jim if you have to, but it isn't necessary."

"Uncle Jim, wow."

"Umm, Mr. Summerhill—" Rose spoke up.

"That goes for you too, Rose. Call me Jim.

"All right...uh, Jim. It's just that there's one little fly in the ointment. I don't know Person Number Three very well but—" her tremulous voice trailed off.

"Can we still share the modular?" Kelly asked, knowing it was the prime question remaining in both of their minds.

"Ladies," Jim sounded exasperated, "I said this before and I'm going to say it again, but it is the last time, so listen up. I don't care what you do as consenting adults in that modular or anyplace else, for that matter. As long as you don't scare the horses or spill the pour, I don't care. Got it?"

"Got it," Rose said, her arm slipping behind Kelly's back.

Jim gave them a last flustered look and then turned his attention to Dave. "As for you, Dave, you haven't checked the accounts in two months. I know you came up expecting a party but I just got a tax bill that I can't sort out—"

"Well," Dave said, relieved at the opportunity to perform a task that proclaimed everything was back to normal at Summerhill Foundry, "we'd better go take a look at it." He grabbed the handles of Jim's wheelchair and wheeled him from the room. Alice, in her unobtrusive way, had already left and so Kelly and Rose found themselves alone on the couch.

"Whoa," Kelly said. "My brain is reeling."

"Mine, too."

"Kelly," Dave was back in the living room. The moment her head snapped up, Dave tossed something that, glinting, flew through the air and landed with a clack at her feet.

"What is this?" Kelly bent over to retrieve the item.

"Your truck keys."

"My truck keys! Holy Toledo, Rose. I have a truck. And a family."

"Then, my dear, whoever-you-are, let's take that truck and get out of here."

Dave laughed at Rose's remark and then was gone again.

"Why do you want to get out of here?" Kelly murmured seductively. "So you can find out who I am?"

"No, stupid, so we can go get some dinner and get our heads back on straight."

"We will never be straight, honey."

"No," Rose agreed, standing. "That's true."

Kelly stood also. "How about that Chinese place where I first seduced you?"

"If I recall correctly, it was I who seduced you."

They were already walking out the door. "But," Kelly demurred, "you thought I was someone else at the time so it doesn't count."

"It does too!" The door slammed shut on Rose's outraged rejoinder. Alice, not giving away whether she had heard it or not, came quietly into the room to clear away the punch bowl and take down the hearts.

Three years later on a windy spring day, a life-sized bronze

EPILOGUE

of Nancy Summerhill, leaning forward into the future with her arm slung around Barbara Knox's back, was lowered into place by crane and its base riveted to the concrete pad that had been prepared for it.

The women would look out forever upon the red and black lava escarpments of the *Caja del Rio,* the timeless blue backdrop of the Jemez mountains and the silent blue-green waters of the Rio Grande where they flowed into the deep well of Cochiti Lake.

The memorial included a plaque and it had been dedicated not only to Nancy and Barbara but to all those who had lost their lives in the lake or in the river through misadventure or human violence.

Punch and cookies had been set out for those friends, relatives, and officials attending the event and when the monument had been set in place and the first curious raven lighted on Barbara Knox's shoulder, a representative from the Arts Council cut the ribbon swathing the pair and let them fly forever free.

Kelly and Rose stood with Jim and Dave and Alice, their faces to the wind just as Nancy's and Barbara's were. "I still love this place," Kelly said. "It's beauty sinks into my soul every time I come here."

"I love it even more now," Rose said, gesturing at the bronze to which she and Kelly had devoted thousands of hours of intense labor.

"I agree," Alice said. "They belong out here. I never knew either one of them but they only heighten the beauty of this place. What do you think, Jim?"

"I love the bronze. All of you know that. It's perfect and it celebrates them. Even so—"

Dave looked down to see tears filling Jim's rheumy old eyes.

"What is it, Jim?"

"I'd so much rather they were alive and here to laugh with us today."

It was impossible for anyone to speak after that so no one did, but Rose slipped her hand into Kelly's and squeezed it and together, they faced the wind.

Melting Point **by Cleo Dare**

Cover Illustration: Eyewire.com, design by Meredith Elkins

Interior composed in Desdemona and Book Antiqua type faces with Adobe Woodtype Ornaments, using Adobe PageMaker version 6.5

Printed by Thomson-Shore, Inc. on 50# Joy White Offset 444 ppi stock

ORDER FORM

Complete the form below, providing credit card information or including check or money order, and mail to:

Women's Work Press, LLC
Order Processing Center
P.O. Box 10375
Burke, VA 22009 - 0375

Please Print:

Name ______________________________

Address ______________________________

City State Zip ______________________________

Phone Number ______________________________

Credit Card Number ______________________________

Expiration ______________________________

Signature (required) ______________________________

Qty	Title	Price	Subtotal
	Melting Point by Cleo Dare	$12.95	
	Beware the Kiss by J. Alex Acker	$12.95	
	Death Off Stage by Carlene Miller	$12.95	
	Cognate by RC Brojim	$14.95	
	Virginia residents, please add 4.5% sales tax		
	Shipping: $5 for first title, add $1 for each additional title ordered		
	Total enclosed		

On-line, secure ordering is also available at www.womensworkpress.com

We will never sell, rent, or share your personal information with anyone.

How Still My Love

by

Dianne McGavin

Toni and I met on, of all things, a blind date. Add to that the fact that we double dated with a married couple, and that we had to be coerced into meeting each other, and it makes for a very interesting story to tell our grandchildren someday.

Of course, my arm had to be not merely twisted, but practically torn from its socket to agree to it initially. Just because someone is your oldest and dearest friend doesn't mean she knows what the hell she's talking about when she says she has what's best for you in mind.

Apart from sounding horrifyingly similar to my mother—except for the fact that my mother never tried to set me up with women—Jen was and is my oldest and dearest friend. Having met early on in our college years, we became virtually attached at the hip almost immediately. Jen knows everything about me, even things I don't know myself. Or so she often attempts to convince me.

"What else have you got planned for Friday night?" Jen fidgeted while I ignored her query.

"See? Absolutely nothing! Just as I suspected. You have no excuse not to go."

I set my pen down and glanced up, although I knew that was exactly what she wanted me to do and I was in no mood to comply with her wishes. She was smirking, almost as if she was reading my thoughts.

"Jen, I'm trying to get some work done here. My bills aren't going to pay themselves."

"You're not going to get any work done until I leave, and I'm not leaving until you say yes." She grinned sardonically, leaving me to wonder why I had ever sought her friendship.

Just then, it appeared that I might be saved by the bell, figuratively speaking, when Stuart returned from his lunch break. His massive figure stood in my doorway, his mouth upturned in a wide smile beneath his graying goatee. Seeing Jen, who was now part of the extended family my design team had become, because of her frequent visits, he greeted her warmly.

"What are we trying to convince the boss to do? I'll help," he offered devilishly.

"Oh no," I huffed.

"Yes! Why didn't I think of this before?" Jen shrieked. "Stuart, you're the perfect person to help me convince her! I'm trying to set two beautiful women up, but one of them is being adamant about not letting me do it."

They both stood near the doorway, glaring at me. I knew then that I had lost the battle.

"What's wrong with you? I'd be honored if Jen would find a handsome young gentleman for me to date, hint, hint. It's not like she's selling you into an arranged marriage or anything!" Stuart had made his point. It was my turn to glare.

"How often do blind dates go well? Name one couple that is together today because of a blind date," I argued.

"Dan and I," Jen replied.

"You liar! I happen to know you hounded that poor guy until he finally asked you out!"

"Look," she began trying another tactic. "You won't be alone. Dan and I have a babysitter lined up and we'll be with you. Come on! You know we never get out any more!" she pleaded. I recognized the guilt trip before it was completely out of her mouth, having heard a similar plea many times before.

"I'll be your babysitter, then you and Dan can have an evening out alone. Or if you really feel the need to provide an evening out for this friend of yours, have her babysit for you!" I suggested playfully.

Stuart had returned to his art desk, but I could see that he was hanging on every word, ready to jump in and add his two cents if Jen needed him, although I think he could see at this point I had no choice but to give in.

"Can you at least tell me where we're going so I'll dress appropriately?"

"I thought we could go to dinner and a movie. We can go shopping tomorrow for something for you to wear. Your wardrobe consists of jeans, tee shirts and business attire with nothing in between. None of those will do, I'm afraid."

I sighed with an air of resignation. It was clear who was in charge of Friday evening and I just hoped it wouldn't be a waste of my time and money.

For the first time since the date was arranged, I found it difficult to keep my mind on work. The tension was immediately noticed by Stuart and Chris, who showed no hesitancy in teasing me tirelessly.

"What time would you like me to have the U-Haul at your

place tomorrow?" Stuart asked at one point. His expression was so serious that I didn't catch on to his little joke until I heard Chris laughing breathlessly. Earlier, he had called me over to view his computer monitor to look at some wedding invitations he had designed on his lunch break. If I hadn't felt the amount of affection that I did for them, they would have been job hunting that very afternoon.

The dragging hours ticked by until five o'clock thankfully arrived. Chris cleaned her work area and stopped by my office before calling it a day. I looked up to find her moving toward where I sat at my desk.

"I know we've been giving you hell with our remarks all week. I'm glad you're a good sport." She moved closer and reached around me, enclosing me in a great big bear hug.

"Have a great time tonight," she wished.

"I'm sure I will. Thanks," I answered, returning her hug.

After inspecting my watch for what was probably the tenth time since I'd left work, my nerves became more frazzled and I was instantly sorry I had checked at all. I was almost completely dressed but my hair was wet and I needed to apply makeup. Searching around the bedroom, I gathered up my shoes and slid them onto my tired feet, reminding myself to never again agree to anything like this after a full day at the office.

I stumbled into the bathroom and worked some mousse into my hair, examining it closely in the mirror as I massaged the foam over my head. I frowned at my reflection as I noticed that I should have had the color touched up. My head was covered in sunshine-tinted golden locks, but the roots showed my natural dirty-blonde secret.

I grabbed the hair dryer and tossed my hair wildly, attempting to dry it quickly. This alone would take ten minutes, I was sure.

Not until I pulled my convertible into the first available parking space of the restaurant did I allow myself an attempt at a soothing deep breath. It didn't work. I knew without looking yet again at the time that I was very late and that the second Jen spotted me, I was as good as dead. Giving in and checking my watch one last time, I saw with horror that I was close to a half hour late. I supposed that Jen had convinced herself as well as those with her that I wasn't coming at least twenty minutes earlier. I grabbed my purse, and with my stomach in a tight knot, I locked the car door and headed for the restaurant wondering why I had ever quit smoking.

I entered the restaurant and was immediately greeted by the maitre'd.

"I'm meeting someone at seven. I'm late obviously," I stammered, hoping he could make sense of what I meant to say. "The reservation is under Stevens," I guessed, hoping that Jen would have made the reservations under her own name.

"Yes, they've been waiting," he assured me. "Follow me, please." His coolness did nothing to ease the tension building up inside, tying my stomach in knots. I followed him and noticed them at a table around the corner. Jen was staring directly at me, blankly. If I knew her at all, which I did, she'd been staring at this entrance for the past twenty-five minutes. Upon seeing me, she smiled, relief written across her face, and she waved as two heads turned in my direction. Dan waved also, but I barely noticed. My gaze was transfixed to my date for the evening, who was watching me from across the room, a slight smile directed at me. I instantly forgave my friends for arranging this meeting and rushed forward to be introduced.

"Do you know how late you are?" This, of course, was Jen speaking. "I thought you weren't coming."

"Yes, I do. I'm sorry." I turned to my date and repeated, "I'm so sorry." She smiled then. A great, gleaming smile that warmed me, literally. I could feel the warmth begin in my toes and creep upward, making the hairs on my head stand on end.

"It's all right, I'm sure you have a valid excuse," she offered as she extended her hand toward me. "I'm Toni Vincent." Her voice was as deep and honey-rich as I imagined it would be when I saw her face. It was a throaty rasp that did nothing to lower my body temperature.

"Beth Anders," I shook her hand and introduced myself as Dan stood an held my chair for me.

"Glad you could make it," Dan kidded as he settled back into his seat.

"You need to get a cell phone," Jen insisted, oblivious to everything except that I was late.

I settled into my chair and tried my best to focus my attention on the conversation my friends were attempting to have with me. My concentration kept turning to Toni, who sat next to me sipping her drink. If anything at all about this beautiful woman indicated what she was thinking, it was her dark crystal eyes. Expressive and glistening, they seemed to dance as she watched me, accenting her smile, which I knew was genuine.

"I've heard so much about you over the last few weeks," she was saying.

I returned her smile, and commented, "I'm sorry to say I've heard practically nothing about you." I glanced at Jen, who had a silly 'I told you so' grin plastered to her know-it-all face.

"I don't know if Jen told you, but she has a masochistic streak," I continued.

"She also worries about you. That was evident before you got here," she said gently.

"I knew she would and I should have called. I was just running so behind schedule, then when I finally left the house I found that I was almost out of gas." I knew I was rambling, but continued. "When I stopped at a service station, I got the most attentive gas station attendant you'd ever want to meet. I could go on, but it was just one of those days, believe me."

"I forgive you," Toni answered, her chin resting on her hand as the three of them laughed over the tale of my earlier predicament. I hadn't yet figured out if she was intentionally flirting with me or if she was just naturally seductive.

We were politely interrupted then by the waiter, who asked for my drink order. I found it difficult to take my eyes from Toni to answer him, but I somehow managed. She was also quite a conversationalist, I found, as we talked about a wide range of topics. She would watch me intently as I spoke to her, often placing a stray hair behind her ear while she listened. I tried not to stare, but found her gestures almost hypnotic. Her dark hair fell in long curling locks framing her face, and her lips were full. It was her lips, which outlined her perfect white teeth that caught my attention as she spoke, forcing me to imagine how it might feel to be kissed by Toni.

A Stitch of Love

by

Jean A. Bauer

One day, Victoria brought home a young woman close to Colleen's age. Victoria introduced her as Abigail Hetherton.

Colleen's jealousy was immediate. She wasn't sure what the jealousy stemmed from. Although Abigail stayed many nights with Victoria, Colleen was not jealous of her place in Victoria's heart. On the contrary, she found herself jealous of Victoria. Abigail had awakened the feelings in Colleen that V ic toria had so desperately tried to draw out of her. Before long Colleen's loyalty to Victoria was tested, when Victoria was called away to tend her ailing mother.

Abigail called on Colleen the very day after Victoria had left. Colleen was shocked to find Abigail's feelings were a mirror of her own. When Abigail casually brushed her lips across hers, Colleen felt the excitement travel to the most private areas of her body. This had never happened with any of the young men she had kissed. The tingling persisted long after Abigail left her standing in the doorway. What would she tell Victoria? She felt she had betrayed Victoria's kindness.

Abigail visited the next day and Colleen shared her misgivings with her.

"Don't be afraid of your feelings, Colleen. Victoria has been in this life for a very long time. She was my first love. I'll always have a special place in my heart for her, but as I'm sure you're aware of, Victoria is not a young woman. She's well beyond our age. When I met her, I was only fifteen. She was a friend of my parents. If they knew what Victoria was, they would have nothing to do with her. They would never allow me to be friendly with her."

Abigail frowned while she thought about her parents. "I know they want the best for me, but they don't have any idea how strong my feelings for women are. Getting back to Victoria, Colleen, she brought me into this wonderful life then left me after a year for another young woman. She's a wonderful lover. It's just impossible for her to be faithful. From what she has told me, she never found anyone she felt she could spend the rest of her life with. Colleen, you need have no guilt. Victoria gets tired of lovers. You would become just another of her conquests that she would leave behind after the newness wore off."

"How can ye say that about Victoria when ye're still involved with her?" Colleen's defenses were up.

"Don't become angry with me, Colleen." Abigail's voice was calm and soothing. "Victoria and I have an understanding. After she tired of me, I was devastated when she had another woman." Abigail drew in a deep breath hesitating before she could continue. Colleen could feel the pain she must have felt.

"After some time and many tears, I accepted the way Victoria is, and in between her women, we share a bed. It isn't a life commitment for either one of us. I have also had other women. Many of them have been married women whose circumstances have placed them in a life they are not happy with. They look for women like Victoria and I who are willing to be their little secret." Abigail could feel Colleen's apprehension.

"Don't feel that you would be just another woman to me, Colleen. My feelings for you are deeper than I've felt for anyone other than Victoria. I had to accept Victoria's ways with great reluctance, but it doesn't mean that I want my life to be as solitary as hers. I haven't had the luck to meet someone like you." Abigail moved closer to Colleen and slid her arm around her.

Colleen slowly relaxed, becoming comfortable in Abigail's embrace. Climbing the stairs to her bedroom seemed the most natural thing to do with Abigail.

"I'm not sure I can do this." Colleen voiced her fears.

"You don't have to worry, Colleen. If you don't feel comfortable, we'll stop." Abigail reassured Colleen.

As they stood in the center of Colleen's room, Abigail lightly touched her lips to Colleen's. Once again Colleen felt the tingling sensation. Abigail's lips parted. She gently parted Colleen's with the tip of her tongue. Colleen had never been kissed by anyone with such tenderness. The eagerness behind Abigail's tantalizing flick of her tongue left Colleen weak with a desire to explore the unknown. When Abigail left her lips to pursue her ear and neck, Colleen was breathless. She could feel Abigail's fingers undoing her dress and removing her undergarments.

The continuous licking of her lips, ears, neck, and the exploration of Colleen's breast left Abigail weak with a deeper desire she needed to fulfill. She wasn't sure whether she would be able to stop, if Colleen asked her to. Her doubts were put to rest, as she felt Colleen removing her dress. Their passion mounted with every breath they drew.

Colleen couldn't remember how they reached her bed, but she was quite aware of the feelings of exhilaration that swept over her with each sensation that Abigail was creating in her body. As her body spasmed relentlessly until she could no longer respond, Colleen experienced a spiritual awakening.

Even though her body seemed to have spent itself, Colleen felt the need to discover Abigail in the same way that Abigail had taken her.

Something inside of her seem to take over, when she entered Abigail with her fingers. She found herself licking Abigail's body until she discovered the pink pulsating little button where pleasure seemed to originate. Colleen's hunger only intensified. She ate voraciously with little satisfaction when she felt Abigail's body lurch with the intensity she herself had so recently felt. Colleen was overwhelmed with her feelings.

Their nakedness only seemed to fuel further passion, until what seemed only minutes turned to hours. Finally, both exhausted with pleasure, they fell into a deep restful slumber.

Abigail woke first to the sunlight streaming through the small window onto Colleen's milky soft skin.

Feeling Abigail's eyes upon her, Colleen lay still while she remembered her pleasure. Colleen knew now that what Victoria had wanted of her was her destiny. The guilt she was feeling was quickly put aside as she felt Abigail's lips brush gently across her own. She was sure she would find the words to tell Victoria. Feelings of strength quickly faded when she heard voices from the downstairs rising to her room. Although the voices seemed closer, Colleen realized they were just very loud and excited.

Jumping from the bed, Colleen's guilt returned like a heavy burden. Before Abigail could recover her shock at Colleen's rapid exit, Colleen was dressed and headed for the door.

"Colleen!" Abigail almost screamed. "Where do you think you're going without your shoes and me?"

Abruptly Colleen turned to shyly look at Abigail.

"So it's guilt we're feeling, is it?" Abigail read her look with trepidation.

Hanging her head and almost whispering, Colleen tried to deny Abigail's allegations. "I'm not feeling guilty." She swallowed hard. "Yes, I am. How else should I feel with all that Victoria has done for me?" Raising her head to look at Abigail, Colleen's desire returned. The voices from below broke her confusion. As her hand reached the door, Abigail reached for her. The kiss combined with Abigail's nakedness erased Colleen's guilt.

Breaking from their kiss, Abigail kissed Colleen's neck and whispered in her ear. "I love you and I think you love me." She didn't wait for Colleen's answer. "Our love will find the way for us." Tenderly she kissed Colleen again.

Reluctantly they parted, when they heard the approach of footsteps. Silently Abigail grabbed her clothes and tried to dress quickly. The rap on Colleen's door startled neither of them.

"Colleen? Colleen?" The cook's booming voice screeched, while her rap was thunderous. Colleen waited for Abigail to complete her dressing.

Opening the door a crack, Colleen could almost feel the cook's distress before she even knew it's source. "My goodness, whatever is the problem?"

"Oh, Colleen. Miss Victoria has taken ill." Cook continued in an excited state. "They're bringing her up the stairs right now. Her mother's died and left her with the sickness. You must come to take care of her."

While cook grabbed her arm and pulled her from the room, Colleen was slow to react. Abigail was left behind to wonder what she should do. When she heard Colleen call, she ran from the room anxious to see whatever was wrong with Victoria.

The men were carefully placing Victoria on her bed when Abigail reached Colleen's side. She so wanted to place her arm around Colleen. Victoria's face was a deep reddish pink covered with perspiration.

"She's got the fever, Mum." Cook was as flustered as Abigail had seen her. "We'll all be dead in no time."

"Why don't you go down and fix the mistress some of your best broth?" Abigail ignored cook's dread and doom statement. "We'll take care of Miss Victoria." She ventured a glance at Colleen as cook was leaving to do as she was told.

Sorrowfully staring at Victoria, Colleen didn't even notice Abigail's eyes on her.

Gently removing Victoria's clothes and replacing them with fresh bed clothes, Abigail took charge of the situation. "Colleen, help me roll her over." Colleen remained fixed to her position by Victoria's bedside.

"Colleen!" Abigail raised her voice, shocking Colleen from her reverie. "Don't listen to cook. Some people never get the fever." Abigail tried to reassure Colleen.

The guilt Colleen was feeling was almost more than she could bear. While Victoria was tending to her sick mother, Colleen had been falling in love with one of Victoria's women. She could only hope to nurse Victoria back to health and ask her forgiveness. Colleen could not help the way she felt about Abigail though. Her dilemma only made her more determined to make Victoria well.

Before cook returned with the broth, Abigail was able to touch Colleen in a loving moment. It was just enough to soothe Colleen's nerves. Fetching a bowl with cool water and a cloth to wipe Victoria's forehead further calmed Colleen.

Trying to nurse Victoria back to health was an unending job, one Colleen was sure she was incapable of without Abigail's help. Colleen was sure she would fail. Together they worked tirelessly around the clock trying to make Victoria comfortable. Wiping her brow with cool cloths, changing her sweat-drenched night clothes, and holding her hand were all they could do. Sipping small amounts of cook's broth was becoming more and more difficult for Victoria as her strength faded like the setting sun.

After several visits from the doctor, the day he walked Abigail and Colleen into the hallway his voice took on a grim tone. "I'm sorry, ladies, but even with all your good care of Miss Lamb, she will not live more than another day."

Colleen broke down in tears. Not from the imminent passage of Victoria, but from the guilt she would never be able to overcome without the chance to talk to Victoria.

The Cheek of the Night

by

Agnes Browne

Penny rushed her mother through the rain to the waiting limousine. There were no sons to perform the job nor even step-sons. Like herself, Penny thought, her mother was all alone in the world. Again.

Once inside the car, Penny shrugged the rain from her shoulders, slicked back her dampened hair and sunk gratefully into the plush upholstery. It was over. They could go home now. True, a neighbor was at the house guarding the 'funeral meats' that friends had provided and no doubt other neighbors, friends and coworkers would still drop by. But the absolute worst was over.

Her mother, Penny assumed, was numb. As the hearse pulled smoothly away from the curb, Penny heard herself blurt out, "So, Mom, what next?"

She could have inquired less crudely, she realized, deciding the rigid formality of the funeral must have finally cracked her composure. But she was empty of the energy needed to berate herself, apologize, or even rephrase the question. What she most wanted to do was slip into a pair of worn-out blue jeans and tattered sweatshirt, loll on her bed munching chocolate chip cookies—not fretting about crumbs or calories—and lose her-

---

self in a sappily-pointless romance novel.

Her mother shifted in the seat and cleared her throat. "I lost two fine men, Penny. But I loved them both."

"I know, Mom." Penny hoped she sounded appropriately commiserative, knowing she had little left in the way of emotional comfort to offer. Maybe a hot scented bath instead of the self-gorging scenario...

"I don't want to mourn this time."

"What?" Penny wasn't sure she had heard right. Was her mother taking an out-of-character stab at stoicism? Connie Burt—she had informed Penny she was going back to her maiden name in fairness to both husbands—was not a person who repressed her emotions.

"I know I'm old—"

"Oh, heavens!" Penny expostulated. She didn't want her mother to sink any deeper into melancholy than necessary.

"I meant, Penny," her mother explained, "that I am old enough to know what grief is and to know there's no help for it. Of course it will sneak up on me at moments and I will give in to it. But I don't have to indulge in it. Do I?"

It was a startling thought to Penny. Her voice took on an edge of wariness. "What are you saying?"

"Life is a gift, Penny. It is here for us to enjoy, to relish, to sink our teeth into. The two men God gave me to cherish I have cherished with all my heart. I was married twenty-four happy years to your father, three to Gerald—"

"So?" Penny interrupted.

"So I'm only fifty-two years old."

"And I'm twenty-six. I'm sure you're not trying to impress me with a display of mathematics. What are you driving at?" Even as she asked, the obvious answer struck her with force. "Mother, you must be crazy! They haven't even buried Gerald's coffin yet!"

"Good God, Penny, what are you thinking!" Connie's grief-lined face blanched in horror.

"Hell, what are you thinking?"

"I certainly wasn't suggesting anything unseemly! I was merely going to say that instead of moping around the house or trying to forget the agonies of the last month by loading myself down with extra hours at Melissa's Sundries Shop, I should take a few weeks off. Go somewhere silly and unimportant. Take a vacation. Reabsorb life." Connie's voice cracked on the word `life'.

"Oh." Chastened, Penny settled back against the seat. "Well, that's okay, then. It's probably even a good idea."

"Great," her mother sighed, relieved. Then she dropped her verbal bombshell, which despite the plushness of the hearse's interior, imploded in Penny's head.

"I want you to come with me."

"Nobody's from Poblazon, New Mexico," chided the dark-haired man looming over Penny, his voice friendly and amused. His hands, the fingers long and tapered, sat astride his slender hips and his mustached grin revealed perfect teeth. Penny felt her face flush as she bent her head to take a hasty pull at the straw bobbing around in the foam of her piña colada.

Connie Burt smiled at the young man and leaned forward, a strawberry daiquiri clutched in her ringless hand. "The remarkable part is that, 3000 miles from home, we run into someone who's heard of it."

"Yes," Penny agreed, her composure restored, "who told you we were from Poblazon?"

"The ship's purser. He knows I'm from Poblazon and he

pointed you out to me. See him over there?"

"You're from Poblazon?" Connie asked, giving only the briefest glance in the direction of the purser.

"I apologize for my rudeness at not introducing myself." He extended his hand to Connie. "I'm Raimondo Cortez. My dad owns Cortez Hardware."

"Juan Cortez! Of course. I've been in his shop many times. Well," Connie said, releasing Raimondo's hand, "won't you join us?"

"I can't," Raimondo apologized, his dark eyes flashing at Penny as he extended his hand to her. "I have a show in forty-five minutes."

"A show?" Penny was puzzled. She shook hands, noticing Raimondo's grip was firm and warm.

"Yes. I'm the stage manager for some of the ship's evening shows."

"You work here?" Penny's voice rose in surprise.

"Yes." Raimondo grinned. "Someone has to do it. I'd be delighted if you came to see it this evening. Perhaps I could join you for drinks afterwards."

"Mom?" Penny turned in her seat.

"It sounds lovely. We've been shopping in San Juan, we've been to the shipboard cinema, we've played Chinese checkers and shuffleboard. But we haven't been to a show yet."

"I promise you won't be disappointed." Raimondo executed a small bow. "It was a pleasure, ladies."

Penny watched Raimondo cross the vast carpeted expanse of the M.S. Copacobana's Seafarer's Lounge until he was lost to sight behind a set of swinging doors.

"Well, well," her mother remarked, her eyebrows raised and her voice heavy with speculation.

"Mom," Penny warned, "don't start playing matchmaker

on me."

"Someone has to do it," Connie teased, recalling Raimondo's words.

"Mother!"

"Honey, when was the last time you dated someone? Even casually?"

"You know I've been working my butt off getting my bookkeeping service underway!"

"Penny, you know your work isn't preventing you. It's your father. You need to let him go. You need to live again."

Penny shot a look of sharp anger at her mother. Connie returned it with a gaze of steely defiance. "Well?"

Penny dropped her eyes and viciously jabbed her straw against the convex bottom of her empty drink glass. Piña colada foam had stained the sides of the glass with sticky patterns of gold-white bubbles.

"Poblazon is so small. I don't think there's an available man in town."

"The bright lights and big city of Las Cruces are only forty-five miles away, dear."

"I haven't had the energy," Penny muttered, smothered in an uneasy wave of recognition of the *ennui*, the grim routine, the 'going-nowhere' quality of her life.

"Sweetheart," her mother offered, leaning forward to pat her on the knee, "maybe you'll find someone here."

"On a cruise?" Penny snorted. "Were only here for a week! How would that constitute a relationship?"

"Who said anything about a relationship? Just take advantage of the opportunity to be social, get out of yourself—"

"—and sleep around?"

"Oh, darling," her mother sighed.

"I suppose you think," Penny demanded, rage twisting her stomach, "that Raimondo would be a good choice?"

"He does come from a good family," Connie agreed.

"That's it, Mother!" Penny slammed down her glass on a side table and leapt from her chair. "I'm going back to our cabin." She trounced away and Connie watched her go, making no move to chase after her.

As furious as she knew she had just made her daughter, Connie wasn't feeling regret. She believed—meddling as it was—that it was going to take a bit of pushing to get Penny out of her rut. And the child was in a rut. A five-year rut.

Penny's grief for her father had continued unabated from the day Henry died and Connie knew the horror of the event and the aftermath of the loss had stopped her daughter's life in its tracks. Admittedly the circumstances were tragic but Connie believed enough time had passed since that dreadful day.

She remembered it with crystal clarity, especially the strained phone call from her traumatized daughter. Penny worked with Henry at the commercial garage and towing service which was his pride and joy, sometimes performing mechanics, but mostly handling the bookkeeping, the errands, and the parts runs.

Coming back one ebullient spring day from a lunch run bringing sandwiches and sodas to share with her father, Penny had discovered him crushed to death beneath a failed hydraulic car lift.

In the months following, Connie closed down Henry's Garage, selling off the car lifts, the wrecker, and the tools. But the property stood vacant and unused on Highway 10 going out of Poblazon. A paint-peeling and fading 'For Lease' sign hung tacked to the wall but, despite the years, Connie had received no offers.

A tear leaked from Connie's eye and she brushed it firmly away. She too had mourned and the emotional trauma was not healed but she had forced herself to move on. She had met Gerald and started over.

But Penny...what was it going to take to jump start her life? Connie knew that falling in love was the most effective of all antidotes for grief. Unfortunately, no one could force such a happenstance. Leastwise, mothers.

Connie Burt shrugged and downed the remainder of her drink. Nonetheless, it couldn't hurt to hope.

Penny stripped off her white blouse and tan slacks and flopped down on her bed in her underwear. The tiny cabin was stuffy with the accumulated heat of the day. She laced her hands behind her head and stared angrily at the claustrophobically close ceiling.

What was wrong with her mother anyway? Even if Penny did find someone interesting on the cruise, where did her mother think she was going to bed them, to put it crudely? Their shared cabin was the size of a postage stamp and their bunks were narrower than her own twin-sized bed at home.

Really! Penny was exasperated. It was bad enough she had to call the eight businesses she normally visited the third week of the month to balance their accounts and tell them not to expect her—which meant she'd have piles of work to catch up on when she got back—but on top of it her mother was trying to run her social life.

Okay, she admitted, she didn't have a social life. But she was sure she could if she wanted to. At least, she thought she could. Couldn't she?

Was her mother right and she'd been out of the game for so long she didn't know how to approach anyone? She certainly felt inept and awkward and she chided herself that she was too old for either emotion.

Penny thought back over the previous seven years and found the recollection a painful one. She'd only dated a few times in her last two years of college with nothing serious developing and then she'd gone to work for her father at the garage. She'd gone out a few times before her father died but felt no spark of kinship with anyone.

Afterwards...afterwards, she'd really had no energy. She lived at home and, ironically, watched her mother date. Her mother had dragged her to a few political and community events before she met Gerald but Penny had always felt like a fish out of water. Especially if her mother was being escorted by a new companion. Then she wasn't just a fish out of water, she was a decided third wheel.

Other than sympathy and curiosity, she had gotten little attention from men. It was almost as if she was a marked woman. She was certainly a mute woman. She had no idea what to say or do on a date.

Discussions of her work, while comfortably familiar to her, bored males to sleep in less than two minutes. She wondered if her drab asexuality had gone on for so long that she now gave off some stench of loneliness that scared men away.

Or was it that she just couldn't let go of her father as her mother had implied? Was that it? She had energy for work. Why didn't she have energy for men? When she was with one, even one making a heroic effort to romance her, her interest level hovered around zero.

Maybe her mother was right. She should let herself out a little, try to be socially engaging, take a chance. Maybe, just maybe, the right man was aboard this ship. All she needed to do was look around and find him.

She thought back to Raimondo. When he'd come up to them, she'd felt more a sense of trepidation and embarrassment than libido but maybe she was just out of practice. Maybe he would grow on her.

At the very least, he seemed like a good place to begin. He was from Poblazon, after all. At least they had something in common they could talk about.

Penny got up from her bunk and slipped out of her bra and panties. She headed for the tiny shower, feeling a flare, if an admittedly restrained one, of enthusiasm. She would dress elegantly for dinner, attend the show, and then let Raimondo ply her with drinks. Who knew where it might lead?

Penny sat beside her mother at a small round table in the darkened show lounge, crowded closely about by other merrymakers. At the moment, they were watching a dazzling dance line of long-legged ladies dressed in sequined bodysuits of flaming pink and orange, their heads sprouting feathers in the style of Las Vegas showgirls.

But because the cruise line guaranteed family entertainment, the costumes and the choreography were carefully free of salacious content. The show tune to which the women were twirling and bobbing and waving was from the musical 42nd Street, reprised by a small live orchestra.

Penny was mesmerized by the shifting colors, the upbeat tune, and the shapely legs. She tried to prevent herself from enjoying it too much, having in mind the notion that all such displays were somehow degrading to women, but found it strangely pleasant to watch anyway. The dancers seemed in such bright happy contrast to her own dull existence and mousy demeanor.

Penny shifted in her seat, remembering she was supposed to be making an effort to appear confident and sociable. She banned the image of mousy from her mind, remembering that even she had thought she looked good in the simple black shift she had chosen for the evening. She had piled her shoulder-length hair on top of her head and teased a few blond tendrils into twists to trail down in front of her ears. Gold hoops dangled from her earlobes and delicate gold chains graced her bare neck.

The music came to an end, the dancers vanished and Raimondo, looking silly—to Penny's mind—in a silver-sequined tuxedo came on stage and, after demanding extra applause for the orchestra, announced the next act.

It was a magic act, the final event of the evening, and Penny hardly paid attention to the name of the magician, who walked on stage with a flourish. He was wearing a top hat and tails and the requisite white gloves and waved Raimondo away as though he was no more than a noisome fly.

The magician started with standard magic fare, drawing first handkerchiefs and then flowers from his sleeves. His patter was polished and he was rewarded with both laughs and scattered claps from his audience. Penny looked on, boredom creeping up on her. She glanced around the room, seeking anything else of interest, but could see little in the dark.

With a snap of his fingers, the magician drew her attention back to the stage. A large painted box was being wheeled out. The magician twirled the box around, opening it and showing it to the audience from several different angles. Interpreting by the audience's murmurs that they were satisfied the box was empty, he called for a volunteer.

"Preferably a beautiful woman," he shouted, his voice heavy with suggestion. There were laughs and titters. Penny looked to her left, over her mother's head, and saw that a woman was indeed mounting the steps to the stage. It was not until the woman had crossed the stage and stood smiling and shaking hands with the magician that Penny realized she had been holding her breath. She let it out and stared.

The woman was striking, with glowing copper skin and lustrous cinnamon hair that tumbled in waves around her oval face and down her long back. She had lustrous almond-shaped eyes, high round cheeks and a slow sexy smile that made Penny feel her body was melting down into a pool of warm wax.

She was wearing an evening gown of emerald, the bodice plunging low across her full breasts. The sequined-sprinkled fabric shimmered at her trim torso and firmly hugged the curves of her buttocks and hips, ending daringly at mid-thigh. Penny's eyes traveled down the woman's shapely legs to her feet, arched elegantly in glossy open-toed high heels.

Something twisted low in Penny's abdomen and she uttered a groan. Her mother turned to her in quick concern.

"Penny? Are you all right?"

Penny, her mouth feeling like cotton and her tongue like a block of wood, took a quick swig of her Seven and Seven and swallowed it down. "I'm fine," she whispered, shocked that she had groaned out loud.

She looked back at the stage and saw that the woman was being helped into the box by the magician. His gloved hands supported hers and the woman smiled kittenishly at him as she settled herself into the box. Penny felt a flash of irrational jealousy.

With his subject inside, the magician latched shut the box lid. The woman's head, her hair cascading to the floor like a shimmering waterfall, and her feet—dangling from the other end of the box—were the only parts of her body visible to the audience.

The magician resumed his patter but Penny heard little of it. She was absorbed by the beauty of the woman's profile: the smooth line of her high brow, tapered nose, dimpled cheeks, and full lips.

Penny recalled the famous trick called for cutting the woman's body in half. The magician, after he had accomplished this gruesome feat, would separate the box into two sections to prove he had in fact done so.

It was an illusion, of course, and Penny knew how it was done. She was well aware that the feet extending from the box were those of a second woman—shod in high heels exactly matching those of the audience 'volunteer'—who had been hidden in the box before it was brought onto the stage.

Even so, she felt a shudder of horror as the magician raised the unnaturally large saw over the box and began to slice downward. Only a man, she thought in disgust, would even think of such a sick trick.

Her absorption was interrupted by a tap on her shoulder. "Hi," Raimondo whispered, slipping into the empty cafe chair beside her. She turned an ashen face to him.

"Hey," he soothed, jumping to the correct conclusion about her distress, "it's just a trick. He isn't really going to saw her in half."

"I know that," Penny hissed back. "Who is she?"

"Which one?" Raimondo, like Penny, knew how the trick was performed.

"The audience volunteer."

"Oh, my sister."

"Your sister?"

"Yeah, she's not really a volunteer. She's Sam's assistant. I got her the job."

"Who's Sam?"

"The magician. Weren't you paying attention?"

Penny glared at him. "What's your sister's name?"

"Edwina."

"Edwina," Penny breathed and nodded her head, as if the name confirmed something for her. Raimondo's brow furrowed but Penny didn't notice. Her attention was riveted on Sam.

He had finished sawing and, with a flourish, separated the box at the saw line. The audience oohed its delighted approval. Sam reconnected the boxes, lifted the lid and, to much clapping, Edwina rose unharmed, and stepped down to the stage, her face creased with a brilliant smile.

Holding Sam's hand, she bowed and Penny gawked as Edwina's breasts shifted forward and their full weight strained against the fabric of her gown, making dark and strangely exciting the hollow of cleavage between them.

Penny's breath caught in her throat and she felt the floor waver beneath her. What was going on? Had she had too much to drink?

Beside her, Raimondo was clapping. On the other side of her, her mother was clapping. But the sound of their clapping was muted, as though she was observing them from a great distance. She sensed that everything in her life had changed, suddenly, in an instant.

But what, she asked herself, what had changed?

The lights came up in the show lounge and Raimondo was standing over her, holding out his hand. She stared up at him, her mind a blank.

"Did you still want to get that drink?"

"Uh," she replied dumbly, getting to her feet. She looked back at the stage. It was empty. Around her, other guests were pushing back their chairs and rising, laughing and talking, sauntering out of the room.

"Sure. Of course. Mom?" She turned to her mother and her mother flapped her hand indulgently.

"You two go enjoy the evening. I'm going to check out the shipboard casino."

"I'm sure you'll enjoy it," Raimondo said, his expressive eyes alight. As dazed as Penny felt, she didn't miss Raimondo's covert signal of appreciation to her mother for their release.

Surrendering to the inevitable, Penny accepted Raimondo's hand and allowed him to escort her from the room.

About Women's Work Press

Women's Work Press, LLC is an independent press devoted to publishing works by, for, and about lesbians. We're in business for a very simple reason: a majority of the books published today do not reflect our lives. Many of those that *do* speak to our experience are poorly written, trite, or formulaic. We're changing that — one book at a time.

We want to create a literary world where there is no need for publishers like us because lesbians are so—dare we say it—commonplace we don't merit putting the adjective "lesbian" in front of everything we do (lesbian chic, lesbian sex, lesbian music, etc.).

We intend to produce romances, sure. Romances that are longer, with more interesting characters and plots that move beyond the "Am I or aren't I?" dilemma. We also intend to bring you works of science fiction, adventure, fantasy, mystery and horror. It's a big world out there, and there's a place for us in it...Let's show ourselves and the world at large that our place is not in the closet, or between the pages of a cheesy lesbian sexcapade, or in those made-for-boys lesbian sex flicks.

That's why we want to hear from you. Our on-line questionnaire, located at http://www.womensworkpress.com is available for feedback and comments. Or, you can send us a SASE, and we'll send you a copy.

Did you like *Melting Point*? Let us know! Send us an e-mail at feedback@womensworkpress.com. To contact Cleo Dare directly, e-mail her at cdare@womensworkpress.com. We welcome all opinions, so don't hold back.

To comment the old-fashioned way, drop us a line at:

Women's Work Press, LLC
Attention: Feedback
P.O. Box 10375
Burke, Virginia 22009-0375

We'll be posting reviews on the web site, and who knows—your comments might appear a book cover some day!

Thank you for giving us this chance to entertain you. We hope we've exceeded your expectations!

What are you reading?